Seacity Rising
A Tale of Unwatery
Adventures

Elika Ansari

Black Rose Writing | Texas

ISBN: 978-1-68433-267-0
PUBLISHED BY BLACK ROSE WRITING
www.blackrosewriting.com

Printed in the United States of America
Suggested Retail Price (SRP) $18.95

Seacity Rising is printed in Century Schoolbook
Photographer: Adam Miklos
Illustrator: Olsi Tola
Cover Artist: Anastasia Yatsunenko

Harmony makes small things grow,
lack of it makes great things decay.

-Sallust

Seacity Rising

A Tale of Unwatery

Adventures

Chapter 1:
Something Terrible

Two round eyes peered out stealthily from under a craggy rock in the very depths of Seacity pond. They shifted left, then right; up, then down. A slimy green head bulged out, followed by a squiggling, slender body. The coast was clear, and that could only mean one thing. It was time for another one of Babak the frog's underwater adventures.

It was an evening like any other in Seacity; an average sized pond in an average sized grove in a location unknown. With the sun almost gone, little light penetrated the water, which meant that the frog had to make do with paddling in the twilight. He kicked his clammy legs through the water like motorised oars, making hoops of lather as he pushed his way forward.

Schools of catfish, sunfish and bluegills

were scurrying home in clusters, shopping baskets dangling from their fins, loaded to the brim with crusty weeds, crunchy lily pads and other groceries for dinner.

Just above the frog, a bale of turtles was plunging downwards from shore, having taken full advantage of the sun's warm embrace while it lasted.

"Hullo!" Babak called out as they swam steadily closer to the seabed. The turtles nodded politely in response, before retiring into their craggy homes, which basically consisted of rows of holes carved into rocks sprouting unevenly out of the ground.

Babak himself lived in a more secluded area of Seacity, so it was always a delight for him to wander through the city centre and observe families, friends and neighbours mingling, exchanging their how-dee-dos in the mornings and their hey-diddily-das in the evenings.

Coming up just below him, Babak glimpsed a mummy and baby koi fish exiting a round, pebbled complex extending upwards from the seafloor; Seacity's one and only library. The little koi fish was holding a tiny book between his front fins, while chattering about it to his mother.

"And then, the hero, Rostam, meets the Princess Tahmina, and they fall in love. And then there's a war and Rostam defeats everyone. Everyone! And then he fights with this other man, Sohrab. Oh, but did I mention Tahmina and Rostam had a son?"

'Rostam and Sohrab.' Babak knew the story very well. In fact, he knew every story written in every book ever shelved at Seacity Library. You see, when he wasn't out and about pretending to be an explorer, the frog spent most of his days at the library, reading. He read avidly about Seacity's greatest legends, but also about heroes and explorers from other worlds. He knew all about the fastest tortoise on earth who had won every race he had ever run in; the country and city mice who were so different yet so alike; and the hard-working ant and the lazy grasshopper who had dared to dream too big and paid the price.

Babak loved stories about anything, but above all, he loved stories about adventure. Perhaps because he thought the most adventure he would ever have himself was through these imaginary heroes. Or perhaps because he secretly hoped that one day, maybe, he would have an adventure of his own. A real one. With real places and real live creatures from lands and ponds of the unknown.

Except - and here the frog sighed - he knew himself too well to conclude that he was not fit for a life of adventure. He was neither brave enough nor driven enough to be a real explorer. He scared too easily, and he liked the comfort and safety of home too much to ever leave it. That is why his make-belief adventures had to do - for now, at least.

Lost so deeply in his thoughts, the frog did not realise that he had wandered too far away from civilisation. Only once he looked around and sensed the waters had turned colder around him, the surroundings darker, and the silence eerier, did he notice where he had clambered into. Dark End: Seacity's very own junkyard.

"Oh dear!" the frog gasped as he scanned his horrid surroundings. Garbage was piling on the seafloors around him; anything from rusted cans, to rotting plastic. Discarded trash that something or someone kept throwing down into Seacity had heaped up in the corner and was starting to decay into a pungent grey mush.

But Babak had come too far to turn back now. "What's that Frogerty, is it treasure you seek? Then treasure we shall find!" he called out to the vast darkness ahead. There were times Babak pretended to be out with heroes of old, like Frogerty the Great. It helped him feign bravery whenever it was lacking.

Honestly though, he would have welcomed a friend to share his explorations with, but you see, he wasn't very good at making friends, and being the only frog in the entire pond certainly didn't help matters. So the imaginary ones had to do for now.

Gloop, gloop, gloop. An unfamiliar sound resonated in the darkness, making the pretend hero stop short. Suddenly his new-found bravery abandoned him. He looked around and saw nothing, but the noise had been enough to trigger the memory of rumours the frog had heard about Dark End. Hadn't someone mentioned something about grimy ghouls and sludge monsters beginning to take form in the heart of the filth? And wasn't this about the time of the night when they were supposed to be roaming the waters, looking for the cleanest of creatures to engulf in their soily grasp?

Babak gulped. His nose twitched as he imagined the stink of their attack, making him wonder, for a moment, whether he should call it a night and turn back. And he would have done it too, if it wasn't for the thing that very unexpectedly caught his eye.

Somewhere among the thick growth of twisting weeds; somewhere between the clefts and cracks of the moss and mud covered garbage, this *thing*, whatever it was, glinted sharply, even through its shrouds of dirt. Almost as if in a trance, the frog trod towards it cautiously and pulled at what looked like a small, corked, crystal vial lodged between the rock's cracks. It slipped out with ease like it had been waiting to be found. Jammed inside the vial was a piece of rolled-up tree bark, which, when uncorked and unfurled read:

'Heed the words of the Water Gods: something terrible comes to the pond. Something that will catch you off guard, and destroy you all, against all odds.'

Puzzled, Babak continued to examine the rest of the scroll, which read:

…………..:::..:::. …: ::..: ;;;..:;:;;

:,;,;,.;,:.....................:.:.:
:...............:..:...........;..;.,;.,;.:......:;

"Dot," he mouthed, perplexed, as he recognised the language of the Water Deities, which only the sacred could decipher.

He let his eyes wander back to the words he could actually read: *"destroy you all, against all odds."*

What did this mean? What was coming? Was Seacity in danger? So many unanswerable questions swished around in the frog's head as he grew wan and quailed.

Babak considered his next move gravely before reaching a decision. He had no choice but to bring his discovery to the attention of the King, the holiest of all Seacitians. If anyone knew how to read the rest of the prophecy or what to do with it, it was him.

Without wasting any time, he re-corked the scroll, bid farewell to his imaginary hero, and swam as swiftly as his little arms and legs could carry him through the foamy bubbles and buoyant tufts of plankton, towards the looming silhouette in the distance.

Sitting conveniently in the very middle of the pond's floor, the Royal Palace took up almost a sixth of the length of Seacity and a fifth of its width. Though it officially belonged to the Royal Family, it also housed dozens of other creatures from the King's Court who had been blessed by the Water Deities and therefore placed under the protection of His Majesty. In fact, as legend had it, it had been the Water Deities themselves who had built the Palace in the first place, with hundreds of thousands of tiny, white seashells that composed its architecture. In its proximity, one could certainly sense their sacred power still bearing largely in every shell that made up its tall, majestic towers and every stone in its long, overshadowing walls, glittering like bijou pearls under the moonlight. Gaping up at the Palace certainly made one feel small, and one that was already small feel even smaller.

Panting, Babak finally arrived at the open archway that led into the courtyard. He then steadied himself and headed across the yard towards the double doors and into the Palace.

He stopped short when he glimpsed two newts standing sentinel on all fours at each side of the doors, guarding the Palace entry. Babak's gaze dropped; body stiffened, and his breaths spluttered out in strained puffs.

He let his eyes wander up again and, yes, there they still were. Not much besides their spindly outline and their long, dangling tails were decipherable in the dimness, but Babak was quite certain it was them. Josie and Bosie; notorious schoolyard bullies and the reason why the frog had a perplexing phobia of all things cubic shaped, though you would think he would have grown accustomed to it after being shoved inside all those lockers day after day.

Though Josie and Bosie were a few years older than Babak, they had been in the same class, due to their sheer aversion to being good students and their aim to promote that aversion among their peers. They were, in fact, due credit for why the frog always underperformed on 'Name that Sea Critter' class tests; he had certainly learned his lesson after the first time achieving full marks and getting a sore beating for it. And why he had pretended to be sick for days after once having just made a narrow escape when he'd accidentally blurted out they were very nasty creatures. And why he had ultimately been *expelled* from school after being unfairly blamed for a very rude letter the teacher had received, signed in Babak the Frog's name.

And now, here they were, guarding the entry to the Palace, each with a pike in one grip (which also had the sharpest spearheads the frog had ever seen). Who in the name of the Water Gods had thought it a bright idea to arm these bullies and put them in charge of the King's safety? Babak harrumphed indignantly.

He had half a mind to turn back while he still could. But no- this was important, and he could not- would not- let his childhood traumas get in the way. He steadied himself, took a deep breath, and stepped forward.

"Halt," commanded the first newt, as both pikes snapped together forming a rigid 'X' to bar the entry.

"Well, well, who do we have here? If it isn't little, slimy Babakins."

"Babak," the frog mouthed, shrinking.

"So how have you been, B?" Bosie smirked. "Last we saw you, they threw you out for that awful letter you sent Ms Bloom. Poor thing, she was so heartbroken."

"That wasn't me!"

"Hey kid, we believe you. It's not us that

need convincing, ya know."

Babak felt embers kindling in the pit of his stomach and smoke flaring out of every gaping hole on his face. *Remember what you are here to do,* the voice of reason weighed in. *Right.*

"I have a message for his Highness," he said, trying to keep his voice from breaking. "It's from the Water Gods themselves. It's urgent."

"Hmm...I don't know. We better test him and see whether he's telling the truth," said Josie, throwing Bosie a sidelong glance.

Their glaring silence made the frog twitch in disquietude before Bosie spoke again.

"Listen kid, these two pikes here, they're not just regular pikes," he said matter-of-factly. "They're magic. Blessed by the old Seer herself. They will be able to tell if you're story's real or not."

"We just have to put it right here, like this," Josie chimed in, lightly puncturing the frog's quivering little abdomen with the spearhead. "And if you are telling the truth, the pike will drop down on the floor of its own accord. But if you're not, it will lunge itself straight into your gut and that will be the end of you."

"Now stay still," said Bosie. "And don't be nervous, that makes it worse. They don't always get it right."

The frog swallowed hard and shut his eyes as firmly as he could, his heart doing somersaults for fear of the cold metal of the spearhead slicing through him at any moment.

Just as his heart was ready to explode out of his heaving chest, he heard one of the newts break into a snigger. He opened his eyes and saw the severe expression on their faces had faded and transformed into amusement.

"Alright, that's enough" sneered Josie, urging his friend to lower his weapon. "Look at him, he's shaking, the poor thing."

"You can go through now," snorted Bosie, as they unhinged the bolt on the doors and thrust them open.

The frog flushed a hot shade of red, realising he had once again been made a fool of. Babak scowled and, for a moment, considered chastising the newts for having made such a spectacle of him at such a critical time. But thinking better of it, he shook it off as best as he could, dropped his head indignantly and made his way through the double doors into the vast Palace hall.

Eight crystalline pillars were distributed across the hall, stretching high into the sky. While the four pillars on the right-hand side and the middle helped hold up the structure of the entire second floor of the Palace, the pillars on the further left side of the hall were merely decorative, as there was no actual ceiling above them. The design made the use of gates and doors somewhat pointless, as anyone could just swim down into the halls from the roofless opening whenever they pleased. But this was not to say that anyone ever dared do such a thing, as all Seacitians knew too well that that was no way for decent folk to seek an audience with the King.

And there in the midst of the hall stood a pearly, full-scale statue of the God Dolphinus, looking hefty, robust, and fearsome. His body twisted into a half circle, splintering through the waves that threatened to hold him back. His chalky fin, flippers, and fluke had been sculpted with the utmost care, with curving contours then sharper on the edges, and His beak spread into something between a chiselled smirk and gritted teeth. And then there was the gaze; etched with such detail and intensity that it bored through the hall like a laser beam pulverising crystals with little effort.

Seacity was peppered with tributes to the Gods and Goddesses they worshipped. In fact, one rarely turned a corner without encountering a bust of the Goddess Crabite, an effigy of the God Sharkus, or a prayer stone to the Goddess Octopette that the pond creatures touched once a day for good luck. The Seacitians were a deeply religious society, existing only, they were convinced, thanks to the protection of their Deities.

Babak bowed his head instantly as a sign of respect and mumbled a quick prayer under his breath as was custom in the presence of the Gods, before circling the statue, wading his way across the hall, and letting himself in through another set of double doors, these ones already propped open, into the Throne Room.

Amethyst walls with hints of purple, violet and lilac meshed and blended together, and aquamarine agate pillars engulfed the King's Court. Finely grated white sand stretched across the foyer like an extended rug, cushioning every footstep. Around it, council members, chamberlains advisors, messengers and even jesters were mingling and jabbering incessantly.

Above him, at the far end of the room, white pebbles were positioned like stairs, one on top of another leading up to the dais where a shiny red can, flattened for comfort, stood as a throne. And there was the old turtle himself, perched majestically atop it, with his oversized shell protruding from the edges.

A smaller, much younger turtle, stood on all fours by the King's side on the podium. Princess Dolores looked lovely in her large crimson hat, elegantly embroidered with gold sequins all around its flat surface. Her hat brought out the single red stripe on the side of her head, while the gold sequins flattered the yellow lines spread unevenly across her hands and legs.

A slightly bigger turtle with a somewhat larger chocolaty shell stood on her right with a golden satin scarf loosely wrapped around her neck. Lenore was slightly older than her cousin, and very independent for her age - a quality Dolores very much admired in her.

Lenore's parents had passed away long ago, leaving their only daughter in the care of her uncle, the King. The two turtles had grown up more like sisters and best friends than as cousins. So alike and almost inseparable, they had nicknamed each other Lee and Lo.

Babak had been in such a flustered state that he had almost forgotten he was looking up at the Royal Family.

He cleared his throat and curtsied somewhat awkwardly in an attempt to correct his previous behaviour, for fear it may have been mistaken for insolence. Hearing no response, he looked up again to see that no one had taken notice of his presence. The court was busy flocking around the room, surely discussing many important matters, but none, Babak thought, as important as the one he was about to present.

Babak cleared his throat once more, this time much louder, and curtsied again. That was enough for everyone to fall silent. His heart began to pound in his chest as he felt all eyes on him, even though he was still looking down at his feet.

"What is it, son?" croaked the old turtle King amicably, breaking the quietude.

"Majesty, my name is Babak Frog. I apologise for disturbing you at this late hour, but what I have to say could not wait until the morning," bellowed Babak for the whole court to hear, still unable to bring himself to look up.

The frog presented the corked crystal vial he had been hiding in his grasp and held it up to the sky for the crowd to see.

Everyone gasped.

He finally brought himself to peep up at the swarms of faces staring at him, most sceptical, but some curious, even excited, to learn what it was that he held in his hand. Silence.

"Well, speak frog!" cried Lenore, who could take the suspense no longer. "What is that in your hand?"

The frog hurriedly uncorked the vial and fished out the scroll, unrolled it and was just about to read it out when suddenly he was interrupted by loud snoring. Everyone turned their gaze to the dais to see that none other than the King himself had fallen asleep!

His Highness meant no disrespect of course, but it was way past his bedtime and besides, a tendency to fall asleep at the oddest moments was common for a turtle his age. The Princess who was standing conveniently by his side, her eyes glinting like liquid emerald, nudged him awake.

"My apologies," drawled the King.

The frog held up the unfurled parchment again, and the throng gasped again, this time more for dramatic effect, in case the King had missed it.

"Majesty, it says that something terrible is coming to Seacity pond."

"Something terrible like what?" spoke the King, sounding less alert than he should have.

"That I don't know," the frog admitted

awkwardly. "I am afraid I can only read the first lines, the rest is written in ancient Dot."

"The tongue of the Gods?" ventured a voice amid the masses, setting in motion an excited muttering.

"How do you even know it's real?" Lenore projected her voice over the clatter, somewhat sceptical. "It could just be someone's idea of a joke." This was followed by more muttering.

The idea hadn't even crossed the frog's mind. "I suppose it could be," he stammered, lowering his head in shame. "I just thought His Highness might want to see it."

The few sympathetic faces he had initially spotted in the crowd had now all faded into glaring disbelief. The initial enthusiastic intakes of breath and muttering had now turned into disapproving looks and hushed whispers. Before the conversation could go further, they were again interrupted by a prolonged wheezing sound.

It seemed the recent news had been a tad too exciting for the King, and he had decided to reflect by sleeping on it (or at least that is what Princess Dolores had announced to the court before dismissing them). She had also gracefully thanked the frog on behalf of the

King for delivering the message, before taking the scroll from his hand, assuring him they would carefully consider their next steps.

As he left the Throne room, Babak could not help but feel the weight of scrutinising eyes staring him down. He could not blame anyone for not taking him seriously. Had he really expected them to react any differently? How could they believe a random message in a crystal vial that could have been planted by anybody was an actual prophecy from the Gods? Suddenly he felt both foolish and embarrassed.

He had trusted his heart over his common sense because something in it had told him it was real. The scroll had made him sense something; something powerful and overpowering that had made him feel brave for the first time in his life. He just couldn't bring himself to convey this properly before the King and wasn't it just like him to falter in crucial moments like this one!

Discomposed, the frog swam back to his little abode, shut his eyes, and allowed the night's slumber shove out his insecurities.

Chapter 2:
The Seacity Council Meeting

Morning rushed in with its ardent warmth and nudged the frog awake. It was a seething, stifling incursion of a morning that was becoming more and more common in Seacity as of late, forcing the animals to dig inches deeper into the ground for a cooler refuge against the heat.

In the first few sweaty moments of his awakening, Babak was in a bubble of peaceful forgetfulness, where sultry weather was conveniently his only problem. But it wasn't long before the intrusive images of the scrutinising and jeering animals in the Palace surged back to shatter his stillness. He turned on his back, shut his eyes anew and wished them away.

The frog lived alone in a pit he had dug up for himself under a large rock at the bottom of Seacity. The pit was only just big enough for him to sleep in and just deep enough to squat in, but standing upright was more of a challenge. Aside from a book he'd always borrow from the library, and some kelp he used to cover himself up with on chilly nights, he didn't have any furniture or belongings. In the morning, the first thing he'd always do was to wedge the rock up a few inches with a crowbar that he always kept at hand's length to let some light in.

The place may not have looked like much of a home to some, but the frog didn't need or crave much else and was more than happy in his humble, cosy little abode. And besides, the sand on his side of the pond was extra squishy, cushioning his body just wonderfully, so he really couldn't complain. Though, if he had to be completely honest, it did get lonely sometimes.

Babak had no family or relatives at all, not anymore at least. All the frogs in the pond had vanished one Slumber night many years ago. No one knew what had happened to them exactly. Just that Seacity had awoken one spring, and the frogs were all gone. All except for Babak, who was only a tadpole then.

If something terrible had befallen the other frogs, he wondered why he was the only one to have been spared. He was not sure whether his surviving had been a blessing or a burden; after all growing up without parents to show you the ways of a frog can be very tough for a little tadpole.

Like, for instance, Babak had never learned to hop like a frog. He mostly just marched in a very *unfroggy* fashion on his two slender hind legs. Even his swimming was at times *unfroggy*, as he tended to just flip and flop his undulating body along with his arms and legs from side to side in a synchronised fashion, more like the fish he had grown up observing than any amphibian.

The frog was still so entrenched in his morning haze that he almost didn't notice someone calling out to him.

"Hello?" came the voice from outside. "Is anyone there?"

Casting aside his kelp covers while taking care not to hit his head against the very low ceiling, Babak used his crowbar to jack the rock up a few inches more and peered through the slit between the ground and the rock. A bulky fish, glowing in several shades of yellowy orange and orangey yellow was buoyed up opposite the rock, with a brown satchel stuffed with letters hanging over his body.

"Babak Frog?" he asked, clearing his throat, when he detected the frog's head poking out through the gap.

"Yes?" came the frog's muffled voice.

"You have been summoned to the Seacity Council Meeting. It starts in an hour. The King will be chairing, so don't be late." He spoke in a rather rehearsed manner, without locking eyes with the frog.

"Summoned? Why?" he managed, taken aback.

"I don't know the details," the fish returned dismissively. He shuffled through his satchel and fished out a small bronze coin and dropped it down for Babak to take. "Here is your entry token."

Speechless, the frog hoisted the rock higher and swiftly extended his hand out through the gap but just missed catching the token, and instead watched as it landed on the ground with a clink. By the time Babak had squeezed out of his pit, the fish was already swimming away to make his next delivery.

Babak took the coin from the ground and traced the letters carved into it with his spindly fingers; 'SCC', which must have stood for 'Seacity Council.'

He brooded over the implications of the summon. To the best of his knowledge, meetings were only held the first of each month in the Council Hall, which was located in the West Wing of the Palace's premises. These meetings provided an occasion for Councillors to come together with District Representatives and other important Seacitians and discuss various topics of varying degrees of gravity and urgency that concerned Seacity. But neither was today the first of the month nor was Babak a Seacitian of any particular importance.

Could the summon possibly concern his message from last night? But they had not believed him at all, and frankly, even if they had, why call him back? He had relayed all the information and provided his evidence. Surely, they knew he had nothing else to add? Thoughts clamped down on his mind, to a point where he didn't even realise he had begun wading towards the Council; heart drumming; hands clammy; complexion pallid.

Head bowed, he fought the sun's scorching rays to progress further. With summer far behind and autumn already upon them, the Seacitians could not help but wonder why the days and nights were becoming warmer, not cooler, as was the season's custom.

Left and right, Babak sensed an irregular number of darting eyes and whispers greeting him as he unassumingly made his way to his destination. Babak was used to getting some stares on occasion, but this much attention was uncustomary, even for the only frog in Seacity. That could only mean the news of his discovery must have spread through the pond already.

He was halted mid-struggle by a wonderful scent wafting towards him, which, for a moment, made him forget where he was going. His mouth watered and his stomach grumbled, as his brain worked quickly to identify the source of the scent. It didn't have to work very long as any Seacitian would recognise that smell anywhere; seaweed pie, his absolute favourite.

He glanced up at the large drifting platform overhead to see all the colours of the pond concentrated in that one place. Customers were hustling and bustling and vendors were wooing and cajoling their customers.

"Step right up, folks! The best seaweed in all of Seacity, right this way," hollered one.

"Is your algae roast bland and insipid? Are you tired of hearing the little ones complain about having to finish their dinner? Well, look no further than Herbert's Herbs!" coaxed another.

Of course! Today was Monday, which could only mean one thing; the day of the Floating Market. Every week, Seacity's best cooks, artisans, confectioners, and *herbmongers* came together and set up shop to sell their finest products. Nowhere in all of Seacity, could you find such a plethora of fresh, delicious, divine flavours and aromas all in one place.

As there was nothing tethering down the platform though, the market's exact location was ever-changing and subject to the water's oscillation. So you could very well plan to go to the place you'd seen it last and find it no longer there, then get caught up wandering through all of Seacity with your nose as a guide.

Babak made a mental note to stop by the market on his way back, that was, if he could locate it again. But for now, he had to focus on the task at hand as he snapped back to reality.

"Deep breaths," he told himself as he pushed on through to the Palace, swerved the double doors and made directly for the Agora to his right. It was a rotund outdoors assembly hall, with its circumference lined with marble columns all the way around. Just at the entrance stood a marble bust of the Goddess Squidina, with her bulging bald head gleaming splendidly, and her lips curling into a compassionate smile that bestowed strength and effervescence to all who stopped to stare - just the karmic nudge the frog needed to make it through the day.

He made for the queue which was starting to form outside and waited patiently for his turn, then unclenched a fist to reveal his token to the Ticketmaster, who was buoyed in the gap between two of the columns. A curt nod from the puffy purple fish granted the frog instant entry.

Babak shuffled in with the crowd and stationed himself at a short distance from the podium where the chairman was to take the stand, making sure to avoid the front rows. And to think! That was the very podium wherein Frogerty the Great (the real one, founder of Seacity, not the frog's imaginary companion) had once stood, speaking directly to adoring crowds of Seacitians. He closed his eyes and tried to imagine what he would have said; what his voice would have sounded like.

When the throng thickened enough to fill out every spare inch in the hall, a fish with a large frilly tail and blue and yellow stripes took the stand.

"Ladies and gentleman," she bellowed into the loudspeaker. "It is my distinct pleasure to welcome his Majesty, the King, to preside over today's Seacity Council Meeting."

A round of exuberant flabby clash of fins passed as applause and cheering, which cued the turtle to emerge from behind the drapes; like a prize slowly (very slowly) unveiled. So slowly, in fact, that the momentum began to die down as the King made his way steadily onto the podium and took the stand. Two tiny purple fish rushed in after him, each with a large leaf in their grip, standing at either side of the turtle and fanning away the sultry weather from the King's complexion.

A hush fell over the crowd.

"Good day. Fine day, is it not?" the King paused and waited for the crowd to mumble something in agreement.

"Except," he mused out loud, mopping away the sweat beads on his brow, "I woke up this morning with an eerie ache in my shell. Oh no, nothing too drastic," he hastened to add as he caught a glimpse of their worried faces. "Indeed, I am getting old, and an achy body is nothing unusual. But this was different, more like a feeling, a tingling of sorts. So I asked the Old Seer to be brought to me."

The crowd gasped in response, then broke into an excited muttering.

Babak did not know much about the Seer, except that she was a mysterious creature that dwelled somewhere between land and water (whatever that meant). So mysterious in fact, that no Seacitian had ever laid eyes on her. But for all she lacked visually, the Seer made up for in strange sounds that every Seacitian could attest to have heard at some point in their lives. Sometimes, at nightfall, when semi-dozing ears picked up on strange incantations diffusing through the undulated echoes, it was surmised that the Seer was busy communicating with the Water Gods.

The prolonged beep-bopping, clink-clanking and tick-tocking noises she made were peculiar to those who had no familiarity with the ancient tongue of Dot, and that was pretty much all of Seacity. The only exception was the Turtle King, who was so old, it was rumoured he had been alive as far back as when the Gods themselves roamed the waters, dotting about their business. But being alive for that long also meant he was ageing, and ageing meant some of the things he knew well were beginning to fade and that included his ability to speak, read and interpret Dot. No wonder he had called for backup.

The Seer only ever spoke directly to Seacitians when called upon, and she was only called upon for very serious matters.

Excited whispers had now turned into more audible chatter, bringing the King's speech to a halt.

"Quiet, quiet please!" the blue fish trilled, exasperated, clapping (or flapping) her fins together, and the room obliged. "Go ahead, Majesty."

"As I was saying," drawled the King. "After telling her about the scroll that was brought to our attention by our young friend," he paused to acknowledge the frog with a gentle smile, making Babak even more anxious, "I asked the Seer to kindly interpret the Dot message on the parchment."

The crowd's eyes were peeled on the King, impatient to hear the rest.

"The Seer's exact words were-" he halted again, as everyone held their breath. "I don't know what is coming." They let out a disappointed sigh.

"However," they held their breath again, "the message on the parchment reads: *Of water you all are, but on land, you shall be three. Your answers you must seek from the Old Woman Beyond the Sea.*"

Heads tilted and confused pairs of eyes darted across the room.

"But what does it mean?" someone yelled out.

"It means," the King went on – in a commanding voice, "that three Seacitians are to journey upwards and find out what we need to know from an Old Woman".

"Excuse me, Sire," said the blue fish on the podium, making the turtle tip his head back ever so slightly. "Surely you don't mean leaving the pond and going up to dry land?"

"That is, in fact, exactly what I mean."

More gasps, followed by cluttered chatter.

What the King was proposing was simply unheard of. Seacitians were a very sheltered community. Never had they ever dreamed of leaving the pond for even a minute, and to journey across dry land no less. Everything they had always known, everything they ever needed and wanted was right there under the water.

The only time an animal had ever left the pond, she was said to have returned raving mad. Beltogra the Loon, they called her. She was rumoured to have lived the rest of her days in utter loneliness, muttering ungodly things to herself and to whoever else was willing to listen. Surely, this was not a fate the King now wished upon any other Seacitian?

A cacophonous clearing of the throat sent ripples from the podium throughout the assembly, making everyone fall silent again.

"Your concerns are noted," the turtle droned. "I won't lie to you, there will be perils along the way. But the Gods have spoken. They are trying to warn us, and we must heed their warning. And with that, I am proud to announce the first brave volunteer has already come forward. My very own niece, Miss Lenore."

At the mention of her name, everyone's attention turned towards the turtle who had been standing at ground level next to the podium sporting a lemon-coloured swimming cap which in turn brought out the dashing yellow markings on her neck. Lee nodded firmly with an air of determination before moving up to stand beside her uncle, then hastened to whisper something in his ear before turning to face the masses.

"Oh, my apologies. *Ms* Lenore," the King corrected himself, as his niece grinned and waved at the whooping throng.

"If there are any other volunteers, now is the time to step forward," the King commanded, suddenly more alert than his character tended to allow.

Bodies squirmed, heads cocked and eyes shifted. Glances were exchanged, some eager, others anxious for someone to come forward before giving the King a chance to start picking out volunteers at random.

"It seems to me that this operation, if it were to succeed, would need tremendous brainpower," a voice with an air of timeless wisdom croaked from somewhere in the back.

Masses parted to make way for the one and only Dr Goldberg, a small orange goldfish with a gaping hole for a mouth and two black currants for eyes. His reputation preceded him. Since a very young age, the goldfish had always busied himself with all sorts of inventions. 'Genius boy wonder,' they'd called him. He was always on the look-out for ways to expand the horizons of his scientific research. And this quest seemed like the perfect opportunity to do just that.

"The thought is much appreciated, my dear Doctor," grinned the King. "But according to your own research, your body would not adapt too well to dry land."

"Ah, but your Highness, with my new invention it just might. You leave that part to me," Goldberg smirked craftily, clasping his frilly fins together.

"Very well, then," the turtle conceded.

So far, two of the prophesied volunteers had come forward. The Brains and the Beauty, some might have said. But those who might have said that clearly did not know that aside from her beauty, Lee had quite a reputation for her super reptilian strength and athleticism. She could single-handedly lift and thrust boulders as big as herself halfway across the pond as if they were mere pebbles. And as for her speed, she was the three-time champion of the Seacity Kayak Sprint Race. Ever since she was old enough to pick up a paddle, she was undefeated and, some might even say, undefeatable. So to have considered her as merely 'the Beauty' would have only told a small fragment of the story.

The time had come now for the third and final volunteer to come forward, but it seemed nobody was willing to accept the challenge. Not to mention, the vast majority of the throng comprised of fish, who, unlike Goldberg and his special advantage, could certainly not survive on land.

It was then that the King turned his gaze to the frog, who in turn gulped suspecting what was about to come.

"What about you, son?"

"Uncle," Lenore interjected before Babak could speak. "Do we really need a third member? Goldberg and I are more than capable…"

"Oh, I have no doubt, my dear. But the prophecy said three were to be assembled. And if the prophecy said three, then three it shall be. So?" he glanced back at the frog, expectantly.

"Highness," the frog squealed, trying to project his quivering voice. "With all due respect, I believe Ms Lenore is right to be hesitant. I have no skills like her or the Doctor. Surely, I would only prove a burden."

"Never be too sure of that, son. If nothing else, your body is well suited for survival on land. Besides, I have a feeling you might just play the biggest part on this quest yet." He winked at Babak.

Lee was a little disappointed by her uncle's last remark but knew better than to speak over him again.

The frog remained silent, and that was mistaken for consent. Not that he had a choice in the matter. Once the King declared any wish, it was quickly scribbled down by scribes and converted into the law of the waters. That was why there were so many laws about napping in Seacity, for instance.

Similarly, the law had decided the three of them were to set off in the early morning to seek out the wisdom beyond the pond. Once all was said and done, the meeting was adjourned, and with it, Babak's unlikely fate to venture upwards was sealed.

Chapter 3:
First Encounters

After a few hours of sleepless tossing and turning, anxiety nagged the frog until he was forced to rise from his bed and leave home long before daybreak.

The frog knew he had to get to the Palace before he gave into crazy ideas like running away, so he whooshed through the water like a wraith on a sleepless mission to haunt a vacuum.

At this very early and very late junction in time, Seacity was an indigo haven of solitude. Every Seacitian was still fast asleep in the comfort of their homes, and it would be several hours still before the first of them would begin to stir. Save the distinct silhouette of the lofty Palace and the frog's occasional splattering limbs as they beat steadily against the water, nothing much could be seen or heard.

Just a few more hours and Seacity would burst into life. Food would be cooking, shops would be retailing, schools would be schooling, and Seacitians would be wading this way and that, going about their business.

The frog felt a pang of wistfulness when it dawned on him that he would not be there to witness any of it today; that, in fact, he would not be witnessing it for a very long time, perhaps.

As he drew closer to his destination, the sluggish contours of the newt guards came into view. They were trudging sleepily from one side of the Palace's double doors to another in a synchronised fashion. Just glimpsing their outline was enough for Babak to grow hot as he recalled the awful trick they had played on him the other day. Though, admittedly he felt more irked at himself for having fallen for it at all.

One of the newts glanced in Babak's direction as the frog came to a stop just outside the courtyard. Too tired to take full notice; however, the newt simply dropped his head and continued plodding listlessly back and forth, counting down the seconds to the end of his shift.

Moments later, the double doors were thrust open, and a large semi-round figure akin to a turtle's shell lumbered through them. The darkness must have been playing tricks on the frog because as much as he strained and rubbed his eyes, the turtle's shell appeared to have doubled in size overnight. A few steps closer and he could see something large strapped across her back. Bigger than her entire shell, a backpack teetered clumsily from side to side with her every step.

Suddenly shaken awake by Lenore's appearance, the newt guards rushed to close the doors behind her and made haste to hurl clusters of formalities, salutes and bows her way as she plodded through the courtyard and came to a stop next to Babak.

"Uncle wanted to see me off, but I snuck out as he started dozing," she said, half to herself.

"My goodness, what's in there?" Babak asked, pointing at the hulk of a bag bulging from her back.

"Water flasks and food mostly. Everything from waterlily cakes to sun-dried duckweed," she responded in a rather impromptu way.

"Chef Butternut Squash insisted. She said we don't know what kind of food they have up there."

Chef Butternut Squash was the Palace Cook and the best-known cook in the entire pond. A plump, rosy stickleback with a taste for exquisite delicacies, she owned a restaurant on East Water Lane, which food critics had awarded five Seashellin stars, making it the most sought-after establishment in all of Seacity. Babak had never been able to afford a meal there himself, which meant leaving the taste of all of her wonderful delicacies to the imagination.

The frog let his eyes wander back to the backpack and tried to picture the tasty goodies hidden inside it. By the size of it, it looked more like whatever was inside was enough to feed all of Seacity for months. His stomach began to grumble, and he remembered suddenly that he had been so nervous all night that he had not even considered bringing any food or anything at all, for that matter, with him.

"Perhaps while we wait for Dr Goldberg, I should go back and gather a few items."

"No time. He should be coming soon, and I'd like to leave before uncle wakes up," Lenore cut him short, seemingly anxious to take off.

They waited in awkward silence for what felt like hours.

"I wonder what Dr Goldberg has up his sleeve this time," Babak felt compelled to break the quietude. "Another delightful invention, I hope."

Lenore jerked her head and twitched uneasily, her eyes darting back to the Palace doors just to check they were still closed.

More silence. Just as Babak opened his mouth to say something else, the sound of a gentle splashing noise made him turn his attention to the round object speeding up towards them.

The frog and turtle started and drew back in fear, covering their faces with their arms. But as the object came to a harmless stop right in front of them, they lowered their arms, stood still and gazed at it in wonder.

"Morning, my dears," came the goldfish's muffled voice from within the object.

"Doctor? Is that you?" the frog enquired dazedly. "Where are you?" He extended his hands in front of him only to be obstructed by a smooth, solid sheet separating the fish from the water.

"Careful with that, my boy," cautioned the fish. Then with a big smirk, he said "This is my new invention. I call it Mobile, as it allows a fish such as myself to move inside or outside the water without ever having to abandon its premises."

As the morning's first sunbeams began to penetrate the water, Goldberg's invention came increasingly into view. It was a round, see-through object, somewhat bigger than the frog and turtle (minus her backpack, that is) and perhaps three times the size of the fish himself. From the outside, two paddles protruded from either side of the object, and four small wheels stuck out from the bottom. The inside seemed to be filled to the brim with water, and other than some buttons, levers and handlebars that the frog assumed made the thing operational, it was decorated with a number of shrubs and even a little cave with a tiny entrance for the fish to retire into for a good night's sleep.

"A Mobile home – how clever!" Babak finally exclaimed.

"Shall we get a move on, then?" Lenore chimed in before her two companions could continue their banter. "It's getting rather late."

With a quick nod, Goldberg grabbed hold of the handlebars and switched gears. Then, fumbling with a few switches here and there, which appeared to be connected to the paddles, he propelled the Mobile into an upward motion. Babak and Lenore followed. The fish rowed while the others swam, at an almost steady pace, moving up towards the inviting warmth of the sunlight.

Once they were at the brim of the pond's water, they poked their heads out (in the case of Goldberg, he poked his Mobile's head out) just far enough to get a preview of which direction to take.

"Oh my, will you look at that?" Goldberg uttered, half to himself. "Truly remarkable." He took a moment to breathe in the view. Though for him what was remarkable was not so much the stretches of fluffy grass, or the stalking trees or the myriad of yellow, red and brown that were meshed together to compose the months of Autumn. Goldberg was more interested in the severed twigs, the fallen leaves or the unexciting shingles on the paths ahead. We might call these the more humdrum parts of nature, but to a scientist, a twig, a leaf or a stone represent a multitude of possibilities.

The frog and turtle, of course, were slightly more familiar with the view than their counterpart, as turtles and frogs both have a tendency to surface every now and then to bask in the sun. But that does not mean they had ever ventured further than necessary to do so. Mostly, the frog just hopped from one lily pad to another, all of which were distributed unevenly across the pond's surface, while the turtle went no further than the rocks on the pond's banks.

"On to Turtle's Rocks!" Lenore called out gesturing at the banks, before swimming ahead, head bulging out, and the rest of her body submerged.

Goldberg's Mobile bobbed back and forth with the gentle sway of the otherwise still waters, as he rowed at a steady pace closely behind the turtle. The frog, on the other hand, dawdled in an attempt to make peace with what he was about to embark on.

"How did I end up here?" he thought to

himself in silence, body drifting in the water. Until yesterday, the furthest he'd ever been from his home was Dark End. And now, he was just about to venture into this actual uncharted land, where so many horrible and frightening things could happen.

But despite the uncertainty, Babak could not help but feel a tad – excited perhaps? No, it could not be excitement, he assured himself. Surely, whatever it was probably had something to do with his nervousness clouding his judgement. Still, he was somewhat curious perhaps, to see what he would find on land; what kind of creatures; what kind of landscapes, what kind of adventures. At the very least, he could admit that all these things piqued his intrigue.

It wasn't until a few more minutes of daydreaming before the frog realised that he had lost sight of Lenore and Goldberg, so he decided to hurry along.

Just as he was beginning to swim dazedly towards the rocks, his ears pronged at a splattering and splashing that was picking up from behind, as if someone was desperately trying to catch up with him. Poor Goldberg must've fallen behind, he thought.

But gazing directly in front of him, he could still make out what looked like an outline of the Mobile at a distance.

"That's odd," the frog pondered. "Then who could possibly be back there?"

He cocked his head slightly around and saw that there was indeed someone trying to catch up with him, but her reasons for doing so were probably much more hostile than Babak had initially imagined.

Babak was frozen still for a moment, gaping at what appeared to be a paddling bird with the ravenous look in her eyes. Her beak was a flashing orange weapon, snapping open and shut as she whooshed closer. The blood rushed to the frog's head, making him tremble all over as the creature gained on him.

He knew he needed to get a move on to avoid becoming bird feed, so Babak started thrashing desperately in the water. His arms and legs were motors powering the rest of his body into motion in a seemingly futile attempt to outrun his chaser.

The bird was on his tail in no time, and then in one lunging swoop, she thrust her beak at the frog's poor little body. Luckily, Babak dodged it and jumped out of the way just in time.

The stubborn creature didn't seem to be done yet, though. She craned her neck to the other side and dove for her prey anew. Again, Babak jolted out of the way. Left and right, Babak kept diving every time the bird made a lunge at him, but the poor frog was beginning to run out of breath.

Just as he was getting ready to give up and accept whatever fate befell him in her jaws, a faint glimmer of a fast rowing object came into view. It was headed straight towards them and rammed right into Babak's hunter, chest first.

The impact shoved the bird back, but it was not strong enough to cause any real damage, so in no time she was back in motion, wings sprawled open, and now more vexed than before, heading this time for the Mobile.

Goldberg hastened to pull some levers, and the flat crystal sheets on the top of his vehicle began to retreat, granting inside access.

"Quick boy, get in!" the fish yelled.

Babak made an attempt to climb on board, but before he could, the bird closed in on the fish and made to lunge his beak through the gap.

In a haze of desperation to save his friend, Babak did something he did not think himself capable of doing. Just as the bird brushed past him, the frog leapt out of the water and wrapped his stringy arms tightly around the bird's slender neck. He clutched and tugged and bit her plumage in an attempt to tear her away from the Mobile.

And it worked! The bird squealed out in pain. Dazed, she stopped short before reaching her destination, giving Goldberg the time he needed to seal himself back in and out of harm's way.

The bird squirmed and wriggled, trying to get the frog to loosen his clasp. Petrified, Babak shut his eyes and gripped on tighter instead, for fear of tumbling off and making himself vulnerable to his predator's fury.

But he couldn't exactly stay wrapped around her neck forever either. What was he thinking, jumping on the bird like that? How on earth would he get out of this one?

Just as he thought that things could not possibly get any worse, Babak felt a biting chill, like gusts of air beating against his face. He scanned his surroundings to see the deep teal colour of the water replaced by a pale sky blue, then swiftly glimpsed down to see Goldberg's Mobile beginning to fade into a small dot.

In a moment of frenzy, the beast had soared into the sky like an arrow and was now hovering way up in the air, flapping her wings and screeching frantically.

For the poor frightened frog, everything became a blur; the blue of the sky and the white of the feathers, churning and meshing together forcibly like a wheel of pastel colours spinning round and round.

The commotion and pressure were too much for Babak's fingers to bear, so they gave way, and he suddenly found himself swishing backwards in the air's currents. But by some miracle, he managed to seize a handful of feathers on the creature's back before being completely blown away.

Latching on, he steadied himself, as the bird jolted in the air some more before diving back down like a javelin. Babak shut his eyes again, anticipating the impending impact that would send him catapulting off with a huge splash. But when he heard Goldberg calling out to him, he opened his eyes to see a small gap had opened up in the Mobile's lid, just big enough for his body to fit into. The frog held his breath, and when he considered he was close enough, he let go of the beast's feathers and let himself fall right through the gap. This happened just as the bird made a splash in the water, making the Mobile bounce a foot closer to shore.

Goldberg then pulled the levers to close the lid fully, and before bird the could gather herself to come back for them, the fish grabbed onto the handlebars, started up the Mobile, and paddled away in all haste.

The frog struggled to catch his breath while wriggling to adjust his body in the tightly enclosed space inside the Mobile. He stole a glance behind to make sure they were no longer being followed and was relieved to see that was indeed the case. The commotion must have been too much for the bird, as she had now retired to the other corner of the pond to groom her ruffled feathers.

"That was a close one!" Babak panted, mopping his brow.

A few more minutes of quiet paddling passed before they reached the bank. Babak was the first to pull himself out of the opening lid onto Turtle's Rocks. They were flat, smooth rocks that led conveniently like stepping stones onto land.

From there, he put one foot gingerly onto the shore first to test its firmness. The sand felt soft and warm between his toes, similar to the sand under water but the grains here were rougher and much drier. Moderately satisfied that the ground would hold his weight, the frog climbed onto the spit of land.

Step by step, he was getting used to the

strange sensation of walking on solid ground. From his feet, he looked up and suddenly caught a glimpse of Lenore sitting in the shadow of a bush of what looked exactly like the blackberry blossoms he had once read about. The turtle's backpack was sprawled out next to her, and her algae green shell, now exposed, appeared to have flattened under the weight of the backpack. She seemed to be muttering something, but as soon as she noticed the rest of the team's arrival, she instantly fell silent.

"What took you so long?" she called out pointedly, in an attempt to conceal whatever it was she had been caught doing.

"We r-ran into a bit of trouble on the way," Babak stuttered, trying not to revisualise the experience. He then composed himself and gripped one edge of the Mobile, and attempted to tug it onto shore somehow. But it was too heavy.

Heeding his struggle, Lenore left her backpack under the bush and made her way to the rocks. Grabbing onto one of the protruding paddles, she single-handedly heaved the Mobile onto the shore next to them. Her unmatched strength never ceased to impress.

Now that the Mobile was safely on the bank, it was Goldberg's turn to turn heads by demonstrating how his invention worked on solid ground. Constructing features for water, an environment he was used to, was one thing; but to move about freely on dry land, something he had never experienced, was quite another.

Naturally, Goldberg did not disappoint. With one lever pulled in and another pushed forward, Babak and Lenore watched in awe as the paddles were hauled up and tucked neatly away on each side of the Mobile, and how in their place, four rotund wheels started to emerge from beneath the vehicle. Then taking hold of the handlebars with his fins, Goldberg switched gears, and the Mobile began rolling forward onto the path ahead.

Even Lenore, who was quite unimpressionable, could not help but gape at how smoothly and rapidly Goldberg's invention was making its way on the dirt road ahead.

Then, inspired to get a move on, the turtle made for her backpack, and fished out a piece of paper from its front pocket.

"The Seer gave this to my uncle," she unrolled a large parchment to reveal a roughly squiggled map. "The scroll you found alerted us to keep heading South *on the road beyond the flaxen-haired field and onto the Green Ruins.* Why prophecies always feel the need to talk in riddles is beyond me." She rolled her eyes.

"Anyway, we'd better get moving. Ready?" She heaved her backpack onto her shell and began to trudge on all fours without waiting for the frog's response.

Babak turned his eyes towards the vast expanse of land that lay before him and really saw it for the first time.

"I suppose so," he gulped, as his feet reluctantly began to drag him through the warm grains of sand that paved a way into the unknown.

Chapter 4:
The Spooky Night

Being on land was less of a shock for his slithery body than Babak would have expected. The sun's rays were hotter here than under water, but not hot enough to inconvenience his subaquatic biological tendencies; not just yet at least. The sand on the footpath felt soft and inviting between his toes, not estranging, and in any case the task at hand claimed the majority of his focus.

From the moment they had stepped over the threshold that separated land from water, Lee, Goldberg and Babak seemed to have developed an unspoken agreement to cover as much track as possible. So they had tread nonchalantly for hours on the monotonously straight path heading South, without so much as even pausing to rest or eat.

But that did not mean the frog couldn't

stop to dawdle and take in the remarkable sights he'd only ever read about in storybooks every so often; to witness for himself the fallen leaves carpeting the ground, like swirls of interwoven crimson and flaxen threads, and to gaze at the looming trees whose bare branches penetrated the pale, blue sky.

If nothing else, land was certainly a motley of vibrant colours, the kind of which one never encountered in Seacity, where even the brightest and most flamboyant hues paled under a few shades of blue filters.

Hearing on land was also a very different experience. Under the water, one had to listen attentively to pick up on even the popping bubbles, or sounds of squirting, sloshing or wading. On land, sounds just intruded into your state of mind, like they had a life of their own. Babak felt humbled by them - sounds like the echoes of the waft of a gentle breeze, which in turn made brambles and branches rustle; like the sound of robins twittering, wasps droning and the fluttering of butterflies' wings, which were paper cranes beating softly against the air. On its own, each sound would be merely percussive, but interlaced, they formed a philharmonic orchestra, a sheet music melody that only worked if all the elements were present at the correct intervals.

And the scents. Oh, the scents! Everything smelled like something, and every something mingled with every other something to create sundries of anythings and everythings that had never been smelled before; like damp, leafy, lavender tea with a humid, woody and buttery kind of twist, sifting through the air. Even the wafts from the Floating Market dwarfed in comparison to this deluge of aromas here on land.

And yet, wonderful though it all was, it was also too vast and too unknown for the frog to feel entirely at ease. The sense of security and comfort that came with knowing his surrounding was no longer a given. Unlike the pond, this world was an infinite expanse of possibilities, with no limits, no ends, and no ability to predict what they would encounter along the way.

Since Babak had volunteered to be Goldberg's hands throughout the trip and collect a few samples here and there for later 'research purposes', as the scientist had called it, he tended to lag behind, sealing a few leafy, herby samples inside tiny vials he had been provided with.

Straight ahead of the frog, Goldberg's Mobile's was at a near-distance, wheeling through the dirt road as smoothly as it had started out. The turtle, on the other hand, was nothing more than a speck by now. She was always in the lead, immune to all distraction, in spite of the massive backpack strapped onto her shell that would have slowed just about anyone down – anyone but Lee, that is. She truly was a great athlete, Babak mused.

As the last dregs of sunlight left the Seacitians and day was gobbled up by night, the sky became a wondrous sight; something not known to the inhabitants under the water. A full moon had emerged to boldly take the sun's place so it would not be missed, and in the process, had given birth to millions of silver speckles that now scattered unevenly across the velvety sky. The day's music had now stilled, and only a chirping, a certain nightly rumbling and fumbling, and drowsiness and yawning filled the air.

Nights were so pitch black under the water, they were almost violet. They were in fact almost as dark as they were tedious, cold, and very, very quiet. But here on land, they were, in a word, enchanting.

For minutes, the frog gaped quietly at the sky, wondering whether it felt as soft and silky as it looked. He knew he could not stand there and marvel forever, but just as he was about to get going again, pins and needles jabbed at his sore feet, making a statement that they were unwilling to drag his spent body any further.

A thick mass of holly lay just to the frog's right. Its clustered leaves seemed to deny entry to preying animals, meaning, he thought, a discrete enough shelter for the night.

"Hey!" he hollered out to Lenore and Goldberg, who kept walking and rolling as if they were wholly resistant to the night's sorcery.

They tilted their heads to see the frog beckoning them to take rest. Conceding that they had travelled far enough for the evening, the two of them made their way into the bush. The Mobile, with some help from the frog, was propelled in through the brambles and the branches and came to a halt in the clearing where the turtle had set her down her backpack.

Babak went to fetch some fallen leaves from around the bush to cushion his body against the ground. By the time he got back, the Mobile's night-light (yes, Goldberg really had thought of everything) was off, and Lenore had already neatly tucked her head and limbs inside her shell for a good night's sleep. They must have been more exhausted than they had led on.

Following their cue, the frog brushed the shingles away from a patch of ground just big enough for his body and lined it with the leaves he had collected. He set a few leaves aside to cover his body should he feel chilly, to simulate his kelp blanket back home.

He tossed and turned at first, trying to find a position cosy enough to resemble the safe compact of his underwater abode. But they were not in the pond, and he would not, for all he tried, sleep as snugly or as deeply as he did there. So he settled for lying on his back and just gazing up into the darkness, waiting for sleep to weigh down his widened eyelids.

The closely packed leaves of the bush

interlaced to form a vault above him, blotting out most of the moonlight, save the occasional specks trickling through the cracks. A hooting and a howling shattered the night's gentle sounds at intervals. Not the most welcoming of sounds, after he had just about become bird food a few hours prior. No wonder he couldn't get any sleep, in spite of his body crying out in pain and exhaustion.

If today was anything like what the rest of the quest was going to be like, Babak was not sure he would survive it. In fact, he was rather certain he would not survive it. Sure, the frog had always had a taste for adventure, but he didn't exactly have a death wish either.

"I'm sure it will get better," he reassured himself, trying to shove the negative thoughts out of his mind. Turning onto his side, he closed his eyes, ready to let the night's sleep wash over him, when all of a sudden, he heard a strange sound.

"Ksssssssssssshhhh."

He sat up instantly. His eyes popped open, and the leaves tumbled off his body.

He sat still for some minutes, listening intently, but could hear nothing else. Surely, his mind must have been playing tricks on him, he convinced himself, as he lied back down to sleep. He shut his eyes again, and exhaustion started to surge in his every limb once more when he heard it again.

"Ksssssssssshhhh."

This time the frog did not think it wise to sit up, and instead huddled up under the leaves, pulling them tighter over his face and body.

He remembered ghost stories he had heard as a child about the strange creatures that roamed the non-watery world at nightfall; the screeching ghouls and listless wraiths and wicked spirits who raided the lands in search of helpless children to drag back into the netherworlds. Worse still were the slithering serpents and cunning foxes and shifty night owls who loved the taste of squirming little frogs like him. Those were certainly more than just stories.

"Ksssssssssssssshhhhhhhh" it was getting louder, and the frog began to tremble all over, inadvertently giving his position away to anyone who sought after it.

That was it. There was no choice but to make a run for it, he decided. So he leapt up in no time and started sprinting aimlessly from corner to corner in the pitch dark. Back and forth; left and right; he ran as fast as his slender legs would carry him, but nowhere could he find an opening between the brambles and leaves; it felt almost as if they had all been sealed to keep him from getting away.

Then, suddenly in his frenzy, the frog bumped into something bulky and fell over. He cringed back in fear, but when the thing did not so much as move, he opened his eyes to see it was just Lee's backpack.

"Phew" – he was about to utter when he heard the noise again; this time louder than ever. "KSSSSSSSHHHHH." It was coming from inside the backpack!

Overcome with a sudden impulse and curiosity, the frog forgot his angst and slowly unzipped the bag and peeked inside. But what he found was not at all a soul-stealing ghoul or a frog-eating snake, but rather a sleeping turtle. At first he thought it was Lee herself, but he was certain of having seen her sleeping tucked inside her shell just behind him not a second ago. He made to zip the bag shut without enquiring much further, but before he could-

"What are you doing?!" Lenore cried out from behind.

"I'm sorry I..."

"Lee? What's going on?" Princess Dolores had poked her head out of her shell and was gazing up at Babak and Lee, who were now standing face to face.

"Princess? I thought you were..." the frog began, muddled.

"I'll tell you what's going on!" Lee interrupted. "This frog has been snooping around in my PRIVATE belongings!"

"I just heard this strange noise," he managed, staring at his feet.

"Oh that must have been me. I apologise. I snore rather loudly sometimes."

"Don't you realise what a mess we're in, Lo? The frog knows now."

"Oh, but he won't tell, will you Babak?" The Princess winked at the frog.

Before he could answer - "What's all this conundrum?" Goldberg had turned on his nightlight and was approaching on wheels.

"Oh perfect, now everyone knows!" Lee moaned.

"Knows what?" said the Goldberg, his eyes suddenly catching a glimpse of the second turtle, peeking out from inside the open bag.

"Everybody, settle down," Lo stretched her limbs out and stepped out of the backpack into full view.

"Lee and I decided I should come along on this quest."

"But why keep it a secret?" Babak ventured.

"Well, we wouldn't have had to, if it hadn't been for that silly prophecy," Lee said, stomping her front foot.

"You see," Lo began to explain, "The day the prophecy was announced at the Seacity Council Meeting, and Lee volunteered to be part of the team, I was back at the Palace none the wiser, just waiting for everyone to return from what I thought would be another boring meeting. But when Father returned and told me about the quest, I suddenly grew concerned. The safety of my dear cousin was all I could think of at that point." She gave Lee a faint smile, which her cousin returned in kind.

"I told Father that I wanted to go as well. I begged and pleaded, but he would not hear of it. The prophesied three had already been selected, he maintained, and prophecies were not something to be questioned. There really is no arguing with Father once his mind is made up so I had to find another way."

"Later that day, when uncle fell asleep," Lee picked up where Lo had left off, "we rushed up to our chambers and plotted how Lo would come along without anyone's knowledge. We threw around a few ideas on how to hide her -some good, some not so good-" (here the turtles exchanged smirks, sharing an inside joke, it seemed) "but nothing seemed to conceal Lo well enough, and that was when the backpack idea came to us."

Lee didn't have to wait for her cousin to continue. The two really had a flair for finishing each other's stories.

"So it was decided that Lee would carry me on her back during the days, while always keeping a distance from the rest of you, so we could speak freely and sometimes even, if the coast was clear enough, let me poke my head out for some air. It was not ideal, but it seemed to be working, up until now that is."

All of a sudden, the turtle's odd behaviour throughout the journey started to make sense. Her eagerness to leave before the King woke up; the way she had always kept in the lead, despite the heavy load on her back, and without the slightest interest in her new surroundings; and, indeed, that time she had been caught talking to herself - everything she had done so far was just a way to keep her cousin's presence on land a secret.

"Look," Goldberg cut in. "I am a man of science and care little about prophecies. What I do care about, however, is the royal offence you both have committed by directly disobeying the King's orders. And now that we know, we are all accomplices."

"We are well aware it is a royal offence, which is why we devised a plan before leaving. Neither my uncle nor anyone else will ever know Lo is gone," Lee retorted matter-of-factly.

Early that morning, when Lee was expected to leave the Palace, the Princess had waited until her father had fallen asleep to leave him a handwritten note, warning him to stay far away from her chambers, as she had fallen ill and was terribly contagious. She had left another similar note on the kitchen counter for Chef Butternut Squash, asking kindly for all her meals to be slid through her pet door.

The two girls had then left a pile of notes with words like *'Thank You'* or *'That was delicious!'* or *'I can feel myself getting stronger!'* in her room, and had stayed up all of the previous night training Lee's pet snail, Dumbbell, to slide the notes under the door slot as a response any time anyone came to pay her a visit, expected or unexpected.

"But what if someone tries to speak to you through the door?" Babak wondered.

Not to worry. The illness Lo had feigned to have caught had left her utterly voiceless, something she had described in gruesome detail in her notes.

"Hmm," the fish mused, not unimpressed by the whole scheme. "And you are certain this snail of yours can keep up the appearances?"

Babak knew better than to question the integrity of Lenore's training or the skills of her beloved pet.

Just as Lee was about to cry out indignantly at the thought of anyone doubting Dumbbell, Lo weighed in. "Rest assured, Doctor. He is a very smart and talented snail. He will not let us down."

And with that, Goldberg and Babak were mollified and promised to keep the turtles' secret. Then, they all decided to make good use of what was left of the night and get some rest while they still could before taking off again at the break of dawn.

Though the frog quietly rejoiced to see Princess Dolores there with them, he could not help but remain somewhat concerned. The prophecy had been breached after all, and unlike Goldberg, Babak was a strong believer in the wrath of the Gods.

He was all but certain, in fact, that it was that very wrath that had befallen the frogs of Seacity, one winter not long ago when they had all just disappeared into nothingness. Babak barely even remembered what his parents looked like anymore – a faint image of a gentle smile hovered somewhere in the back of his mind - that must have belonged to his mother, but he could not be sure.

It was their wrath that had taken his family from him, but it had taken away so much more than that. It had taken away his frogginess, his ability to hop or swim or croak like a frog, all of which remained unlearned as no one had been there to teach him, and that was something he could neither forget nor forgive.

And what if the wrath befell all of Seacity this time? What if breaching the prophecy jeopardised their chances of finding the Old Woman Beyond the Sea? Or worse, what if it meant they could not get back in time before 'something terrible' befell the pond? What if they could not save their home from it, whatever it was?

No, he refused to think of it any longer and taking a few deep breaths, he tried to calm himself by picturing the Goddess Squidina's tender eyes cooing him to sleep. "For whatever is or is not, and whatever may come to be," he murmured to himself. "May your fears be forever drowned in the depths of the bottomless sea." The words of the Water Deities.

Chapter 5:
The Slace

Morning crept in too soon. The frog's heavy eyelids were prodded open by the streams of bright light seeping in through the bush. Taking a hint from the invasive sun, Babak slipped out from under his blanket of leaves and shifted towards the team to bid them a good morning.

Goldberg had already fed from the store of fish food he kept in the Mobile's cave and was now busying himself with its functional features, making sure the levers and wheels were all in order before they continued on their journey. The turtles were sitting in a corner breaking their fast on some spongy water-lily cakes, courtesy of Chef Butternut Squash. Though Babak had never tried the cakes, the sweet scent wafting over and embracing every inch of his face certainly gave them away to be the most delicious thing he had never tasted.

When his stomach began to grumble uncontrollably, Babak remembered he had not eaten anything for more than a day now. Lo giggled at the sound, and the frog stared at his feet, in an effort to hide his blushing cheeks.

"Sit, please," Lo patted the space on the floor beside her. "Have some." She peeled the foil off one of the cakes and handed it to the frog. He nibbled on it shyly at first, then unable to hold himself back, tucked in ravenously. Truly exquisite.

"Can you believe the frog brought nothing with him, Lo?" Lee sneered. Then glancing at Babak said, "What in waters were you thinking?"

"Well, I-I suppose I thought I'd find what I needed…"

"Bah," Lee interrupted. "And how could you possibly know what you'd find here? None of us has ever been on land. It's beyond irresponsible."

"Now Lee, let poor Babak be," the Princess chimed in. "I'm sure we have enough food to last us all quite some time."

Lee simply rolled her eyes and chomped on

her own cake.

Once they had finished their breakfast, they were ready to get back on the road. To enhance their chances of survival, they had unanimously agreed to avoid the open field, given an increased likelihood of encountering:

A. Large land animals they could probably not outrun (no, not even Lenore);

B. Strong winds their little bodies were unable to withstand (okay, Goldberg's Mobile may have been an exception, but there is no 'I' in 'team', he had to be reminded); and

C. All sorts of other big, strong things that endangered the lives of only the smallest of beings.

Now that the turtle was out of the bag – quite literally – there was no need for Lee to carry Lo on her back any longer and as a result, her backpack looked much flatter and smaller strapped across her shell than before.

"Try not to slow us down this time, Frog," Lee scolded, before charging forward out of the bush and into a copse. Goldberg followed on wheels and Babak, on foot.

"I was almost killed yesterday!" the frog said, disgruntled and cheeks flushed.

"And whose fault is that?" Lee returned, without so much as tilting her head back.

Babak felt the anger welling up inside him. He had just about had enough of her snapping at him all the time.

"Don't take what she says to heart," a gentle voice said from behind his shoulder, just as he felt his head was about to explode. Babak was glad to see the lovely Princess Dolores walking up next to him.

"Princes -I- it's just that, I wish she were more like you."

She offered him a gentle smile, and he turned pink in response.

"Lee may well be stubborn at times, but believe it or not, under that hard shell is a very soft heart," she winked as she brushed past him.

"Oh, and call me Lo. We're teammates now after all," she called back before speeding up to catch her cousin up.

Babak's shoulder numbed where the Princess had touched it, and his mind was clouded by her fragrance; a salty, misty, weedy kind of aroma that reminded him of all things nice and oceany. A few seconds passed before the frog could compose himself and start walking again. But Lee's rudeness was not so easily forgotten, and it wasn't long before resentment started gnawing at his heartstrings again.

"Soft heart? Ha!" Babak scoffed at the idea. True, he admired Lenore's strength and speed. He had never met an animal that could move as fast or as steadily, much less one who could do so while carrying another turtle on her back. But that was all he admired about her. Unlike her lovely cousin, Lo, Lee had been nothing but mean to him from the moment they had left the pond.

He would just have to keep his interactions with her at a minimum from now on, he decided. They had a common mission, and that was to save Seacity, but that was all they had in common, and all they would ever have in common!

When he finally caught up with the rest of the team, Babak was surprised to find them halted and lined up in a semi-circle gazing bewilderedly at something just ahead. The copse had curved away from the open path, then narrowed into a mess of spider-webbing branches, tattered trunks, and spiky brambles, so interlaced that their now single trail had become obstructed by a hulking boulder, bigger than any they had seen before. There was no way around it, and it looked much too slippery to climb, so their only option, if they wished to carry on, was to push the boulder forward in the hope that it would open up a gap they could squeeze through.

Lee took a deep breath, then pushed and shoved, but it wouldn't budge. Then Lo and Babak, joined in the effort, while Goldberg just rolled back and rammed into it with his Mobile on the count of three, but nothing worked.

"That is quite a rock," Lo panted, collapsing from exhaustion.

"I'd say, almost as if I ain't one."

"Who said that?" they all said in unison, swinging their heads from side to side in search for the speaker.

"Right here."

They glanced up to see the boulder had suddenly grown a head. Then, his limbs followed cue and cropped up from his sides

Could it be? But surely it was much too big to be a...

"Are you...a turtle?" Lo asked, jaw

dropping.

"Close. A tortoise. Like turtles, but we like to dwell on land, not water. Hermes is the name."

Hermes. Babak mouthed the syllables silently. Something about the way the letters rolled off his tongue sounded oddly familiar. It was as if they had met before, though that could not be, since this was the frog's first time on land. Still, he was sure he'd heard that name somewhere before. Wait a minute!

"Surely, not THE Hermes? The fastest tortoise to roam the earth?"

"That's the one."

"Well, imagine that! Second day on land and we are already meeting a legend!" the frog exclaimed, his eyes roundly fixated on his object of fascination. They all seemed positively curious, all except for Lee, who just sighed and rolled her eyes.

"Always good to meet a fan. What's your name, boy?"

"Babak Frog, sir. And these are my friends, the Princess Dolores of Seacity pond, the Lady Lenore, and Dr Goldberg."

"Seacity eh? That's about a day's walk from here, ain't it? What are y'all doing in these parts?"

"Well, Hermes," Lo began. "We have reason to believe something terrible is coming to our pond, and we are on an important mission to stop that from happening."

"Something terrible?" the tortoise mused. "Don't like the sound of that. And where are y'all headed?"

"South," Goldberg responded.

"Been South, been Souther than South. Ain't nothing there, take it from me."

"Is that where you won in the race against that light-footed, furry beast?" Babak ventured, eyes still wide and unblinking.

"The hare, you mean. That arrogant yapper. Kept goin' on and on about how he was the bestest sprinter there ever was. So I challenged him to a race and well, y'all know the rest. Served him right."

Babak had read all there was to read about heroes and legends, but none had demanded his, sleepless, unwavering attention as much as the adventures of Hermes, the swiftest, most steadfast reptile the world had ever known. If he could admit it to himself, he had hoped, *dreamed*, of one day maybe, just maybe, watching him race.

Lenore rolled her eyes again, but this time it did not escape the tortoise's notice.

"Am I boring you, ma'am?"

"As a matter of fact, you are. You whine about the arrogance of that other creature, but all we've heard so far is how you're the best racer ever."

"Difference being that good-for-nothing hare was lyin'. I, on the other hand, am telling nothin' but the truth."

Lenore could take it no more. "Let's see about that then! I challenge you to a race."

Three of them gasped.

"Lee, no…"

"Stay out of this, Lo."

"And I accept your challenge, ma'am," Hermes replied, simply.

It was not long before they had all moved to the clearing (for the duration of the race, it was decided, they had to make an exception and compete on the open field, given they could not risk any obstacles slowing them down). The turtle and the tortoise were to sprint up from the oak tree, where they were currently taking their marks, to the next nearest tree, which was a few yards away.

The first to pass the finish line -or that root sticking out of the ground like a sore vein- was the winner. Goldberg would stand by the tree and referee, and it was up to the frog to do the initial countdown.

So, without further ado, Babak stretched out his little arm over his head, cleared his throat and then yelled out as loudly as he could, "Ready...set...GO!" He dropped his arm and in a dash, the runners were off on all fours.

Watching them was something quite impressive. Most of us are aware that turtles and tortoises usually have a reputation for being quite slow; but not these two. They seemed a separate species altogether; one that science had yet to discover.

Lenore was agile, determined, and she took the lead at first. Hermes was more about focus; he was fast, but he was also steady. So when Lenore started to get somewhat tired and lag behind a bit, Hermes took that as his cue and sped up. The tortoise's advantage and disadvantage was his size. Being bigger made him heavier and naturally slower, but being bigger also meant every step of his was akin to four or five of Lenore's.

More than halfway now, and they were coming up at the same level. This is going to be a close one, Babak thought, nervously biting his fingertips. And there it was, the finish line had been crossed.

Gasps were followed by anxious faces and round eyes darting from one to the other.

Dolores and Babak ran up to Goldberg by the tree, as the racers slouched, catching their breath.

It was so close, in fact, that - "It's a tie!" the referee announced.

"Well, that settles it," Lo chirped, clapping her hands together. "You are both equally matched."

"Unless-" Hermes mused.

"Unless what?" Lee, who was still eager to prove her prowess, wanted to know.

"We may be equally matched in a race. However, I'm willin' to bet just about anything there is no one on this planet who can beat yours truly in a *slace*."

"A what?" Lee, Lo and Goldberg voiced together.

"A *slace*" Babak, who was more than learned on the subject offered, rather rehearsed, "is like a kind of race, but contrary to a regular race, the winner is not the fastest runner, but the *slowest*. The number one rule being, indeed, that under no circumstances can the contenders stand still, and instead must keep moving, however slowly, towards the finish line at all times. The last to arrive wins." The impressed tortoise gave the frog a wink, making him turn affirmatively pink and giddy.

"A race to determine who is slowest?" Lee sniggered. "That's absurd. Speed proves athletic prowess; slowness just means incompetence!"

"If I may, that's where you're wrong ma'am. A race may well prove ya got speed, but a *slace*, well, that proves something much more valuable. A *slace* proves ya got stamina. And there ain't no great athlete on earth that ain't got no stamina."

He paused, then added, "Y'all know what they say: 'Slow and steady wins the *slace*.'"

The turtle needed no further convincing.

Soon they were all on their marks again. The frog's hand lifted and dropped, and the runners were off.

There were more gasps, followed by some cheering, and shouting and even banter by the thrilled fans. And then came the stunned silence, which eventually meshed and melted into an awkward silence, and then just plain comatose tedium.

Minutes, turned into hours, and hours turned into days. Okay, maybe not *days,* but it certainly felt that way to the now slouching bodies and heavy eyelids of the bystanders.

Never in his life had Babak witnessed two creatures moving so slowly. Every few minutes, the frog would look up to see the contenders had barely moved an inch, if that. It was as if time itself was standing still.

If it was bad for the others, imagine poor Lee and Hermes, and the amount of patience and perseverance it was taking for them to move at such a moderate pace. They trudged and tumbled and plodded and dawdled, and made every effort to slow down.

But Lenore's patience was wearing thin, and self-restraint was not something she had much practised in the past. So finally, unable to contain the sluggardly pace any longer, Lee sped up and crossed the finish line.

That meant the winner was -

"Hermes, congratulations," Goldberg attempted to sound enthusiastic, only half-succeeding.

Babak began to cheer, more because the *slace* was over, than anything else, but fell silent when he saw Lenore's crestfallen face. Her cousin moved up beside her putting a comforting arm around her shell. She was disappointed to be sure, and Babak understood why. This was the first time she had come second in any athletic contest, so it must have been disappointing, to say the least.

Hermes picked himself up and moved towards her, extending his hand out in front of her. "Good *slace*," he offered gently. She gazed at him for a moment, humbled, then took his hand (the fragment of it, as much as her reptilian limbs allowed).

"Congratulations, I suppose," she mumbled. "That was quite a display of stamina." And then, somewhat unexpectedly, both Lee and Hermes broke into a grin and began to laugh it off.

The others exchanged confused looks, then shrugged it off with smirks of their own. As per an unwritten Athletic Code of Honour the others failed to understand, instead of hating each other, the *slace* seemed to have overridden any trace of tension between the two athletes, making them chummier than ever.

The time had now come for the tortoise to tell his story. They sat around in a circle and waited for Dolores to lay out some sun-dried duckweed crisps to munch on in the meantime.

As it happened, Hermes was not from these parts at all. He came from the Deep South, an extremely warm and arid land with heaps of yellow sand, where the sun beat against the skin all day long and burying one's head in the dug-up dirt pits was the only refuge from the unbearable heat. It was getting hotter every day, so much so in fact that the tortoise's species was beginning to disappear as a consequence.

"You see, when momma tortoises lay their eggs, whether they hatch as boys or girls, depends on how hot the sand pit is. Hotter means more girls are born, and cooler means more boys are born. And well, the temperature has gotten so darn bad lately that less and less boys are bein' born."

"Rumour has it, one day a black smog showed up in the sky straight outta nowhere, and it gave off so much heat that all my brothers' eggs cracked. All the boy eggs were gone, all except for mine, that by some miracle, escaped the darn' rays and made it out alive."

Babak stifled a scream, because, wasn't that exactly what had happened to his frog species? Well, not exactly, as the disappearance of the frogs had less to do with the heat than with - um- he did not know what it had to with, actually. But he had, like Hermes, been the only male frog to survive (never mind there were no female frogs left in Seacity, either).

"So now," Hermes continued, undeterred.

"Seems like I'm the only boy tortoise left in those parts. Well, I was at least. Up 'til I ran away."

"Once I was all grown up, I was winked at right and left by lady tortoises. Then they all started asking for my hand. Might sound like a dream come true for some, but it was really more than I could handle. Not only was I not ready for the married life, but to have the future of my entire species lying on my shoulders was just too darn' much. So one night, when all the tortoises were dozin' off under the stars, I decided to run away. Might've well been the cowardly thing to do, but it was all I could do at the time."

"So I ran and ran, for days, weeks, even months, not once lookin' back. That's probably how I got so good at runnin'. That and the few adventures I had along the way. Met some wonderful and not so wonderful creatures that taught me valuable lessons about strength, patience, and even stamina." He stopped to exchange smiles with Lee before continuing.

"One day, I reached an endless stretch of yellow field, with dry rank grass extending boldly into the sky, and once I crossed it, I found myself here - where the grass was greener, the air was chillier, and there were no tortoises like me around. So I decided to stay for a while and think. Being away really can help clear your head, ya know?"

"So what now?" Lee inquired, with an air of concern.

"I suppose the time has finally come for me to go back home," Hermes said, resolved. "The world is a wonderful place, full of fantastic creatures, but nothin' beats the feeling of being with your own kind."

Deeply moved, the others fell into a brooding silence. Perhaps because something about his story very much resonated with their own. They, too, were on a mission and, they too, wanted to protect their people from danger. Perhaps, they would have wonderful adventures and meet whimsical creatures along the way. And hopefully, like Hermes, they'd return in time to save their home from whatever was coming. And maybe, just maybe, one day they, too, would go down as legends; the four brave creatures who saved Seacity.

Dusk approached as the tortoise finished relating his story, leaving them all in speechless awe. After a moment of contemplative silence, Hermes stood up and dusted himself off.

"I should get goin'. I have a long run ahead of me."

"But it will be dark soon, don't you want to wait until sunrise?" Lee asked, flustered.

"Not to worry, M' lady, I always run better at nightfall. It's cooler that way." He gave Lee a final wink and sprinted off into the sunset. They watched as his boulder-like shape became smaller and smaller, eventually fading into the horizon.

A tear welled up in Lee's eye as she continued to gaze at the dust cloud the tortoise had left behind. When she saw Babak glancing in her direction, she quickly wiped it away and cleared her throat. But it was too late. Babak had, even if for an instant, caught a glimpse of that soft heart of hers her cousin had told him about and had suddenly gained a newfound appreciation for the turtle.

"I suppose that's our cue to get going as well, even if to find some shelter for the night," said Lo, putting one arm around her cousin. "Come on."

Chapter 6:
Lights, Cameras,... Mice!

For the next few days, they travelled through tall weeds, keeping out of sight for the most part, until they had reached the field with swards of dry, high rank grass extending into the sky, which they had only found thanks to Hermes' story.

"That must be the *field of flaxen hair* the Seer mentioned," they had realised, before asking the tortoise for specifics on how to get there. And now that they were here, it was taking a lifetime to push and trample through its monotony.

It was Babak who led the way this time, hoping to make up for his repudiated slowness in the past, with the turtles coming up second, and Goldberg lagging hopelessly behind, since it was proving especially hard for his Mobile to stay on track on the spongy earth that kept absorbing its wheels, or the springy weeds flinging against its crystal screen, obstructing its frontal view. The poor goldfish had been slowed down and gotten left behind so many times, that Lee had volunteered to push his Mobile along for some of the way, which she'd admirably done without a single fuss or complaint.

But the hours of walking through the yellow-clad meadow under the sweltering sun were becoming tiring and cumbersome, and not just for Goldberg. The infinite stretches of grass made it harder for them to see where they were going, or how far they had left to go.

Sauntering absently through the meadow, Babak let the crisp bristly swathes stroke his face, all the while wondering what kind of an animal 'the *Old Woman Beyond the Sea*' in the prophecy would be. Would they even recognise her when they saw her? After all, they had no idea what she looked or sounded like. They only knew that she was a mystical creature, who liked to keep out of reach for reasons unknown. And would she be able to help them at all? It all seemed so uncertain, and so did the entire premise of their quest altogether.

But that kind of thinking would not get them very far. So the frog hastened to put the plaguing questions out of his head and trudged along untrammelled as before, when all of a sudden, out of nowhere, a thick, wooden sword, stuck out from amid the yellow swards of grass and pressed up against Babak's throat. The frog stopped short, and so did the others just behind him. He gulped, and his throat stung.

"You may go no further, traveller," said a small, invisible voice.

The gang stiffened, unable to move an inch for fear of their friend being sliced open by whatever stood disguised behind the grass.

"Who's there?" shouted Lee at last.

"I should ask you the same thing," retorted the voice, sternly.

"Please, we mean you no harm," Lo tried to bargain. "We are simply trying to cut across the field."

"You've taken enough from us; our home, our loved ones. You took everything. But no more. This ends here!" The grip on the sword tightened, and Babak recoiled, his heart skipping in nervous beats, and the others followed suit, expecting the worst. Lee, on the other hand, was getting ready to tackle their assailants, and just as she was about to -

"Bravo, bravo, you were all just marvellous!" Two furry little creatures stepped out from behind the strands; one giddily applauding, and the other brandishing his wooden sword, looking timidly content.

The creatures were slightly smaller than the turtles and not much bigger than the frog. From what Babak had read about land creatures, he could only assume from their pointed snouts and full whiskers, pricked ears and long, slender tails, that they were mice. One of them was lined with chestnut brown fur and the other, chattier one, was a ghostly silver colour.

The team glanced at them, and then at each other, still unsure as to whether they were truly under attack or not.

"What is going on?" Lo ventured finally, breaking the silence.

"That, my dears, was what we call acting!" trilled the silver mouse.

"Ak-ting?" Goldberg mouthed the syllables with some difficulty. The concept was not one that was familiar to the Seacitians.

"Performing, pretending, showmanship, call it what you like. You were marvellous, darling," the silver mouse turned to Lo, and she blushed in response.

Lee who was both irritated at their pretence and was also anxious to press on, cut in bemusedly. "So bottom line, we won't need to fight you to cross the field."

"Oh Heavens no, but we can't let you leave yet," the mouse announced excitedly. "You see, we're only minutes away from kicking off our debut play and we'd be delighted if you could come as our guests of honour. Front row seats guaranteed!"

"Get ready to be dazzled by our beautiful and touching story: The Tale of Anoki and Anaba!" At this point, even the quieter mouse could not resist joining in when squeaking out the title.

Just as Babak, Lee and Goldberg were about to kindly decline, Lo asked the mice to excuse them all for a moment and ushered her team to form a huddle a short distance away, where their conversation could not be heard.

"These mice are travellers, they might be

able to help us with our quest," she told them.

"Lo, they put a sword to the frog's throat. They can't be trusted," Lee said simply.

"But you heard them, they were just acting! It's getting late anyway, surely we can afford this slight detour?"

The team was still unconvinced.

Lo weighed in again. "Do you really want to be stuck in these tiresome fields for another whole night?" And with that, she swiftly won Goldberg over to her cause, and the others soon conceded as well, not altogether incurious about the notion of acting.

Once Lo had announced their decision to stay, their furry counterparts had revelled in a trilling chorus, then politely asked the team to follow them to their makeshift theatre. They led the way in a tangent, cutting across the meadow, and it was not before long they finally emerged out of the field into a small clearing.

"Well, what do you know!" exclaimed an enthused Goldberg, his Mobile wobbling through the last bits of grassland. "We're finally out of that mess."

Patches of dried leaves and sturdy logs

were laid out neatly across the firm ground for the audience to sit on. They were set up to face a wide tree stump with a small wooden signpost positioned right in front of it that read, in messy chalky letters:

Presenting: The Tale of Anoki and Anaba

Recycled titbits of purple, blue and green textile were clumsily pasted together to make drapes that dangled from branches haphazardly onto the stump, disguising the stage from view.

The frog and the turtles tentatively took their seats, and Goldberg brought his Mobile to a halt next to them, none really knowing what to expect. Goldberg was fiddling with something in his Mobile, while Lee was looking at the Seer's unruly sketch of what was supposed to resemble a map, plotting the best route to take in the morning. Lo was the only one among them gaping straight ahead, eagerly anticipating the start of the performance.

Babak glanced around the dell to see other strangely, small and wonderfully strange creatures already sitting on the cushioned floor facing the stage, gazing expectantly ahead. He spotted a group of furry creatures he couldn't place. Scanning their faces one by one, he thought some of them looked oddly like mice in some ways, but were, on the most part, much larger. Some of them were busy twirling their large scaly tails, while the ones with black and white stripes lining their faces merely gaped at the stage, curling their mouths into anticipating smirks.

The sound of flapping wings overhead made Babak freeze for a moment, but he thawed swiftly after glancing at the two small (smaller than him) birds with blazing red plumage across their breasts descending into their seats not far from the Seaciatians, while chirping excitedly and joining the ranks of the audience.

One creature he did recognise was the slick green bug sitting on the corner, which just had to be a giant grasshopper. Or was it a cricket? Storybooks were not the best guides to recognising land animals, it appeared, and the frog thought it terribly rude to ask, so he decided it was a grasshopper and that was that.

Finally, the silver mouse that had brought them all to the glade hopped onto the tree stump and cleared her throat.

"Ladies, and gentlemen...Welcome to the first ever production of our newest and best ever play. And without further ado, let us begin!"

Polite applause filled the air as two mice appeared to tug on the drapes until the stage was revealed. Not unlike the drapes, the stage was unceremoniously dressed up in bits of paper-mâchéd cardboard, painted in the greens and blues of meadowed landscapes and a river.

The chestnut brown mouse stepped onto the stage, sword drawn, and facing a terrified white mouse they did not recognise, uttered in the husky voice that had stopped the Seacitians mid-track before, "You may go no further, traveller." And with that, the show kicked off.

What came afterwards, Babak would later remember in fragments; a series of images blurred, like acrylic colours on a pallet, blending and swirling from separate entities, then combining into something infinitely more beautiful.

The tree stump was no longer a tree stump, nor was it merely a stage, but rather it had transformed into Mouse Valley, the home of the First Mice. Similarly, the brown mouse was no longer that meek, quiet fellow from the field, but the outspoken protector and hero of the Valley, Anoki, who was willing to lay down his life for that of his beloved, the brave and gentle Chieftain Anaba, and for all of Mouse Valley.

At one point, the frog felt himself being lifted from the ground and swept away in an eddy of brisk air, then transported into a different world altogether, though he was fairly certain he had not physically moved from his seat.

Like Babak, Lee and Goldberg's full attention was now turned to the performance, and Lo appeared to be entirely rapt, her eyes wide with a mixture of amazement and endearment and disbelief.

Bearing witness to their story was truly a rollercoaster of spiralling emotions. Babak's throat closed up, and his heart drummed in unsteady beats when the Black Death, a River Serpent by the name of Uktena (or a mouse holding up a cardboard a patched up fabric version of the scaly Serpent) smashed out of the water and ravaged all the houses in Mouse Valley. Tears welled up in his eyes when Uktena ruthlessly snatched Anaba away from Anoki's tight, unyielding embrace. But it wasn't until he witnessed Anoki left despondent, with his body splayed across the floor, with his trembling hands covering his fragile face, crying for his lost Anaba, that the frog felt his heart actually snap in three: once for Anoki, once for Anaba, and once for what once used to be their harmonious home, the now devastated Mouse Valley.

By the end, Babak was still in doubt about what had happened, or what would happen to the heroes on stage. He had so many questions, and he was left longing for answers he was certain he would not get. But one thing he was sure of was that acting was the best thing he had ever seen.

When the show was over, and the two mice scurried out from backstage to pull the drapes shut, the sound of fervent applause filled the dell. Lo led among the teary-eyed enthusiasts, clapping harder and cheering louder than anyone. Even Goldberg and Lee appeared to be moved, one nodding with a wide grin spread across his face, and the other clapping almost (but not quite) as fervently as her cousin.

That night the mice invited their underwater guests to sit around in a circle to drink, feast, swap stories and to celebrate their new friendship. It was nothing like the feasts back in the Palace the turtles were used to; for starters because aside from a few crumbs of bread and some wild berries the mice had gathered as small contributions from the audience, there was barely any food in front of them.

Lee had also procured a kelp pie from their reserves, but a few sniffs and twitching noses, followed by wincing and flinching faces told them the mice did not have much of a taste for underwater food. So the mice had kept to their own scraps (but not without first thanking the turtles kindly first), leaving the Seacitians to their own delicacies. And despite the lack of food and grandeur, it was quite possibly the best feast any of them had ever participated in.

"That was a wonderful performance!" Lo began eagerly. "And such a moving story! How ever did you think of it?"

"It's a true story, my dear, with a few tweaks here and there to adapt it to the stage, that is," a white mouse recounted.

"It was the harrowing fate that befell all of us," a second white mouse weighed in, rather dramatically for theatrical effect.

"You see," began the silver mouse, "before becoming travelling mice, we had lived for many generations beside a large, meandering river in Mouse Valley. Yes, there was indeed such as place as Mouse Valley, though you are certainly excused for thinking it was make-belief." He winked.

"But a few months ago, something terrible happened."

"Uktena!" gasped Lee and Lo in a chorus.

"Even worse," continued the silver mouse. "One day we woke up and saw the sun blotted out by tendrils of thick, venomous smog billowing in the sky. A few minutes later, we heard a sharp explosion followed by shrieks from our fellow mice, so we scrambled to the riverside to see what was going on. And, oh, it was horrible! All we could see in our once lucid waters was the Black Death. The river had been tainted by greasy, black sludge that had then surged upwards in the water and was now beginning to flood our Valley. Before long, the river overflowed, and all our homes were destroyed under its poisonous reach.

"The worst part was that some of the mice who had been by the river that day, the mice whose screams we'd heard, had been carried away by the river's currents, and among them, was our beloved Chieftain, Anaba. We searched everywhere for her by the riverbanks in nearby valleys. We figured she might have gone into hiding, or that she might have been injured, or worse. But it was no use. The water gushed ruthlessly, leaving no traces behind."

The silver mouse paused to glance at the brown mouse, who sat quietly in a corner, head bowed, fiddling with his uneaten scraps. She sighed and continued, "Anoki believes she is still alive somewhere, and he has given us all the hope and courage we needed to keep going and search for her until we find her. 'Anaba' after all means 'She who returns from war.' So now we are travelling around and telling our story to all who are willing to listen, hoping word spreads and somehow reaches the right ears."

"But there is one thing I still don't understand," Lo wondered. "Why didn't you just go back to Mouse Valley and rebuild it? Wouldn't Anaba be more likely to return and look for you there?"

"We tried cleaning up the Valley, but we soon learned just how toxic the Black Death really was," a white mouse explained. "At first, when the coughs started, we dismissed them as mere colds, but then, when the illnesses became graver, and we lost a few good men and women, we decided it was time to get as far away from there as possible. It wasn't easy, but we had to face it; that was not our Mouse Valley anymore."

"And we couldn't stay anywhere near it either," the silver mouse continued. "Most of the other mice sought refuge in burrows not too far away, asking other critters for temporary shelter. As for the rest of us, well, I suppose we decided to become travelling actors. And one day, we will settle down somewhere and build a new home, perhaps, somewhere as luscious and verdant as our Valley of old.

"For Anaba-" murmured Anoki, who was now looking up, wiping at his teary eyes and twitching noise with quivering fingers.

The Seacitians were stunned into silence. Up until now, they had believed 'acting' to be mere pretence. But now, to discover the entire story was real- or as real as it could have been-, they no longer knew what to do with the deep sense of grief that had begun to overshadow their initial enthusiasm.

Sleep did not find Babak easily that night. Muted images of the black smog, the sludgy Black Death, and the seamless destruction they wreaked, flickered in and out of his mind. He tried to picture what it felt like to be stained by it, to have your home tainted by it. He tried to imagine its putrid smell and stifling grip on his skin, as it trespassed on his entire body.

Most importantly, he could not help but wonder what the Black Death was and where it had come from. Was it exclusive to Mouse Valley? Or was there a Black Death under every reservoir just waiting to break loose and wreak havoc on inhabiting creatures?

The thought that there might be one lurking under Seacity pond briefly crossed Babak's mind, chilled his bones, and raced through his pulse, before sleep finally arrived, carrying with it unhappy dreams.

Chapter 7:
Tiny Wars

The sun burned a fierce reddish orange overhead, as the risen Seacitians found themselves in a tangled mess of swathes in the flaxen meadow once more. A déjà vu, surely, but it was what it was. Goldberg cursed under his breath as he pushed every button and pulled on every lever to haul his unwilling Mobile along, and Babak, Lee and Lo trudged on as best as they could under the burden of the flaring heat.

They had uttered their thank-yous and goodbyes (some teary) with the mice that morning, but not before telling them where they were headed. To this, the mice had been quick to echo in unison, "The Green Ruins! Why we were there some weeks ago, you're on the right track, just keep heading South on the dirt road once you're across the yellow meadow, until you reach the saddest tree in the world."

The team were all grins after that, as for the first time for a long time, they had felt they were finally getting somewhere on their quest and wasted no time in getting back on the road. Well, all except for the scowling Goldberg who had to be convinced and cajoled to return to the dreaded field once again.

And now that they had been walking for hours, the moistureless air was beginning to weigh them down. How odd for the day to be so stifling in late autumn. The heat was far too much to bear, even for land creatures, but for animals used to spending the vast majority of their time in or under water, it was hardly bearable.

Still, they ploughed on and on, with whatever might they had to make it across the meadow, and emerged finally, triumphantly onto solid ground. And as promised, there it was, the sandy dirt road, stretching long and wide, twisting and turning, curving and bending, paving their way ahead to the Green Ruins.

They tried to go further, really, they did, but at long last, when their pace had slackened, and they could tread no more, they unanimously agreed to take refuge under the cool shadow cast by the large, shrivelling leaves of the willow tree just to their right. Even Lee needed no convincing this time. So they let their bodies slump wearily against the trunk as they caught their breath.

Babak, who came up behind them last, let himself wearily thump into a comfortable squat, and was just about to close his eyes and let sleep carry him away, when all of a sudden, he heard a tiny noise. He glimpsed around, up and down, but saw nothing. Just as he was about to dismiss the sound as a figment of his overcooked imagination, he heard it again, this time squeakier than before.

He had to squint and strain his eyes to see the two tiny black creatures on the ground right next to him. By the expression he could barely make out on their tiny faces and the way they were shaking their minute fists in the air, he could tell they were unhappy, but he could not exactly make out the words in their jumbled rush of exasperated screeches.

The frog called for backup, and not surprisingly, Goldberg, who had cleverly foreseen a situation where they might need help communicating with smaller creatures, came to his aid. The fish retreated into his little cave, and after a few moments of rattling and clanking through whatever he had in there, he procured a compact silver cone, the size of the frog's index finger, through which, he was assured, any sound would be magnified threefold or fourfold.

As per the Doctor's instructions, Babak pulled out the tiny object, elongating it ever so slightly on both sides, and offered it to the tiny creatures to speak through.

"Hey, hey you!! You ruined our sand tower!" the little creatures were saying.

Bedazzled, the frog rose, and his eye caught a glimpse of the tens of little, jutting sand mounds he had failed to notice before. Of course, these were anthills, home to some of the tiniest of all earthly creatures. The blood rushed to his head when he suddenly noticed the sand structure had crumbled under his weight. What he had sat on was not an accidental cushiony heap of sand, he realised, but a tower that had probably taken these ants weeks to build.

"Oh, Dear me, I'm terribly sorry," he offered.

"Sorry doesn't cut it, buck-o!"

"Just be grateful he didn't sit on you," interjected Lee, who was now next to the frog with her cousin.

"Was that a threat?" said one.

"Bring it on, Lady!" cried the other.

"Calm down, now how about we help you rebuild it?" Lo weighed in, trying to diffuse the situation.

"Fine. But you need to follow our design to the dot."

"One grain out of place and we're all in big trouble with the Queen, you hear?"

So began the expedient reconstruction. Plough, pile, pat. Repeat. Sounded simple enough but it was anything but. Every grain of sand had to be positioned in ways both meticulous and calculated.

"All wrong, try again." "That grain is not dry enough." "No, not like that!" The ants kept squealing orders at them, and Babak almost wished Goldberg had not offered them that sound magnifier, because now they had to listen to every one of their squeaky demands, three or four times louder.

Babak was tasked with heaping up sand. Goldberg's handless nature meant he could only offer encouragement by translating the ants' tiny screeches into more humane guidelines for Lee and Lo, who slowly rebuilt the tower from the ground up, while the ants busied themselves to ensure the more minute features were intact.

About twenty minutes into the reconstruction, the ants were no longer satisfied with the sand quality of Babak's heap, so they instructed the frog to gather fresh grains from the uncharted patch of ground on the West side of their anthills.

That was when Babak came across yet another ant, shaking furiously and screeching inaudible words. The frog crouched down and invited the ant to shin up his hand, then brought the little fellow closer to his ear.

"Hey, what are you doing helping *them?*"

"I'm afraid I accidentally destroyed their tower, so we considered it only fair to help rebuild it."

"You fool! They are only building that tower to destroy my colony and you're helping them do it," squealed the ant, aggravated.

"You're not with them?"

"Me? With the AAU? Don't be ridiculous," he harrumphed. "They're a bunch of ruthless bullies. Do I look like one of them to you?"

'Well, you all seem to have a common attitude problem,' Babak said in his mind rather than out loud. Regardless, the frog's curiosity peaked, so he had no choice but to ask, "The AAU?"

"The Alliance of Ants United. Our sworn enemies. I'm from the good colony next door, the UAA: the United Ants' Alliance."

"I'm sure you're exaggerating. How could a mere tower destroy your colony?"

"Exaggerating? HA! Spoken like someone who doesn't know the first thing about war. Clearly, they need a vantage point to keep watch over us. And when the time is right, BAM! They'll be all over our nest, just like that. But we'll strike back, you'll see. We have plans of our own too."

"What plans?"

"As if I'd tell you, so you can go report back to AAU. Just stop helping them, okay?"

And with that, the ant scuttled off the frog's hand, down his leg, and onto the ground, then inched away from the rival colony's turf.

When the frog returned to the construction site, the tower was on the verge of completion. With the help of the bigger Seacitians, the whole process had clearly been faster than expected, and the two ants seemed pleased enough with the results.

On the other side of the tower, a group of ants were convening and beginning to line up into squadrons, while a slightly bigger ant with an air of leadership hurled commands at them. At their General's count, the squadrons started scrambling up the tower and, when at the crest, they clambered onto each other's shoulders to form an ant bridge long enough to reach and breach the nest next door, if that was indeed their aim.

Fear gripped Babak when he realised what he and the others might have unwittingly become complicit in. Briskly, he rounded up his friends and led them behind the willow tree to share his (and the other ant's) suspicions in a hushed voice. They all took a moment to ponder the possibility of a potential war between the ant colonies. Then it was Lo who suggested they should confront the ants directly about their intentions before proceeding any further.

"Friends," Lo called out to the ants, as they re-approached the tower. "May I ask what you intend to do with this sand tower once it is complete?"

"Just tower business, nothing to worry about," the first ant lied softly through the cone.

"We have reason to believe you will be using it for war, and until we know for sure you will not be attacking any other ant colonies, we refuse to let you use it."

"They started it!" The second ant blurted out.

"You heard wrong lady, it's for self-defence," the first, still calmer one weighed in. "The colony next door is stealing our water. We just want to keep an eye on them to make sure our pond remains intact and untouched."

"Pond? Where?" Lee, Lo, Babak and Goldberg exclaimed in harmony.

The ants nodded towards a puddle of rainwater collected at the right side of the willow tree, just on their imaginary border with the rival colony. The Seacitians exchanged discrete smirks as if to say 'Some pond that is.'

A screech was at once heard making them all spin around to encounter another group of ants glaring and yelling at them from behind the ant-made frontier. The UAA, who had been listening in from the other side of the puddle, were outraged by the slanderous words uttered at their expense.

Lee shifted the magnifying cone to their side for the UAA to voice their concerns, "politely," Lo urged.

"Liars!!! We were here first! The pond is ours!"

But sometimes manners failed. The cone switched sides again.

"No, we were here first and our Queen is parched!!"

A raucous exchange of muddled, high-pitched squeals ensued, followed by threats in the form of tiny arms and tiny legs and more tiny legs flailing in the air. Just as the ants from each colony seemed ready to cross the border and start an all-out ant war, the Princess Dolores of Seacity thought it prudent to step in and exercise her diplomatic skills.

"Enough!" she bellowed loud enough to scare the ants into silence. "The matter will be settled without violence." Kind, though she was, she certainly knew how to take a hard line when the situation called for it. Yet another quality Babak secretly admired about her, he thought blushing, then swiftly looking at his feet embarrassed by his own inappropriately-timed distractions.

Lo allowed each side a few minutes to explain their side of the story. It appeared both colonies had been expanding for months, to accommodate their ever-increasing ant populations and their desperate need for water. But it was no easy task to find water anymore. The weather was unreliable; black clouds appeared in the sky on occasion, but rainfall was very scarce. Both colonies' Queens suffered from severe dehydration.

So imagine their joy when they had found that huge pond full of water (here again the turtles, frog and fish exchanged swift glances) and had started digging burrows and tunnels leading directly up to it. They had even built a new Royal chamber and prompted their Queens to move closer to the source of hydration. Only to come back and find these other ants had claimed the water as their own!

Lo pondered the two claims for a moment before announcing her conclusion. "I will meet with the AAU Queen." Before giving the UAA a chance to call her out on her betrayal, she continued undeterred; "and my cousin will meet with the UAA Queen." She glanced in Lee's direction and interpreted her nod to mean she could proceed.

"We will urge both colonies to reach a fair and peaceful settlement," she finished off.

Gasps. Then silence.

"Now, if you please, take us to your Queens," Lee proclaimed.

More gasps, followed by an excited muttering.

It seemed Lo had broken the impasse between the colonies by negotiating a temporary ceasefire, and very cleverly so.

After a brief consultation with their respective Queens, the ants were ready to comply. Luckily, a peephole was already punctured into their anthills, overlooking each Queen's chamber for just such an occasion, so it was only a matter of peeking through it with a single eye and speaking in hushed voices to avoid sending a trembling throughout the entire nest.

"Her Majesty the Queen will see you now," denizens of ants from the AAU and the UAA announced simultaneously.

With a brisk exchange of nods, each turtle proceeded on their mission. Babak and Goldberg, on the other hand, were cordially requested to move ten steps away as this was to be a private meeting.

Moments of silence passed before, Goldberg finally suggested they come up with a Plan B, should the diplomatic negotiations fail. Though Babak had every faith in the Princess's plan, as the ants' screeching got louder and angrier in the backdrop, he relented.

A short while later, a crestfallen Princess Lo trudged back towards them, wearing an irked expression.

"How did it go?" the frog almost did not venture.

Lo heaved a deep sigh before recounting what had happened.

"As instructed, I stared in through the

peephole. Given my constricted view, I couldn't see much besides a large ceramic chamber (large for an ant, in any case), with a white bed wedged in between two corners, and what appeared to be an ant lying buried under the blankets. She seemed slightly larger than the other ants and wore a tiny golden crown on her head."

"I cleared my throat discretely and whispered, "Hello? I am Princess Dolores of Seacity Pond, do I have the pleasure to be addressing her Majesty the AAU Queen?""

"After a brief pause, I heard a faint response."

""Madam. Allow me to extend the courtesies and gratitude of AAU. Thanks to you and your friends, we might finally be able to get rid of those imposters from the UAA.""

""Oh, but I am afraid there has been a misunderstanding," I uttered quietly. "I am here to broker a peace settlement between the colonies, as my cousin is now doing the same with the UAA Queen.""

""Madam," the faint voice came again. "I understand your intentions are pure, and again I thank you for them. But I am afraid the UAA Queen cannot be trusted. She is a vile trickster and has deceived even her own colony. Stories of her are known among ant colonies stretching thousands of nests away. For, you see, she was ousted even from her own colony long ago for her devilish schemes, and she scoffed at them, claiming she was better off on her own. She wandered the earth aimlessly for some time, gathering food, building makeshift anthills wherever she travelled, but before long she grew weak and tired, realising the inevitable: that ants cannot survive without a colony. One day, she happened upon a nest that had just emerged from an ant war. The ants were dazed, confused and too weary to know this from that. That nest was the UAA. So when she saw her chance, she infiltrated their colony by convincing the poor ants she was their rightful Queen and ordered them to murder their actual Queen. She would have done the same to my subjects had they not been warned about her guile beforehand.""

"I was stunned. Never would I have imagined a ruler to be so ruthless. Still, I thought it prudent to stick to the plan, and just as I was about to negotiate further, I heard the tiniest of voices I've ever heard. So I fell silent and tried to listen."

""Mama,... May I go play by the pond?""

"My eye barely spotted the creature, the smallest I've seen so far, waiting by the foot of the Queen's bed."

""No, dear. The UAA soldiers have barred our access."

The Queen managed in between coughs."

""Mama, are you going to be okay?""

""Don't worry about me, dear, you have to be strong, no matter what happens to your mother." the Queen cooed."

"Then the baby girl turned to me. "Please, Madam Big Eye, please help my mama.""

"My heart was in blazes. I had no idea the AAU had suffered so much hardship at the hands of the UAA. And I was not about to stand for this injustice any longer."

""I'll get you your water back if it's the last thing I do!"" I replied, a little louder than I had meant to, sending a quake through the ground."

""Oops, my apologies your Majesty.""

""Think nothing of it, just please, do what you can, for my daughter's sake.""

Not long after Lo had finished her story, Lee came ploughing back with the same disheartened air. There was an awkward moment of silence which none of them dared to break.

"Those UAA ants are conniving tricksters and their Queen is the worst of all!" Lo snapped suddenly.

"My thoughts exactly about the AAU!" Lee

whacked back.

"The AAU Queen has been most patient and forgiving."

"Forgiving? Is that why she's given the order for the UAA Prince to be taken hostage if spotted near the pond? He is just a boy, Lo, and now he can't even leave his nest for fear of being captured!"

"What are you talking about? My Queen would never do that! Not like your Queen, the imposter who had the rightful UAA Queen killed!"

Babak and Goldberg watched the turtles hurl insults at their contending Queens back and forth like a game of ping pong, not daring to intervene. Meanwhile, the ants from both sides had now heard the commotion and were beginning to crowd around the turtles. Before long the UAA and the AAU ants were joining in the turtles in their own Queen's defence.

"Lies, all lies! Stop slandering our noble Queen!" exclaimed the UAA.

"Your queen is deviant! And you're all just doing her bidding!" the AAU yelled back.

What came next among the rise of mangled quarrelling voices, was a terrible upheaval; angry chatter, followed by spinning motion and relentless chaos. The ants rushed wildly in all directions, knocking each other over, while Lee and Lo were too busy squabbling among themselves to notice.

What had ironically started out as a peace mission had somehow turned into a full out ant war. It was time for Babak and Goldberg to shed their uncertainty and step out of the shadows to put an end to this madness.

"Excuse me?" Babak cleared his throat. "Could everyone just listen for one moment. We think we may have a solution."

Not a soul flinched.

"Hello?"

Still no notice.

"ENOUGH!" Goldberg bellowed through his Mobile's loudspeaker.

The fighting stopped suddenly.

"Now, while these two ladies were busy negotiating *peace*," he threw a sarcastic glance in their direction, making them both look away, embarrassed, "the boy and I devised a solution. Tell them, son."

"Well um, see we could build a dam," he uncrumpled a piece of paper to reveal some scribbled notes and what looked like a rough design. "Right in the middle of the puddle -I mean pond. It would split the reservoir up into two equal parts, and by the Doctor's calculation, that should be just about enough water to last both colonies until the Winter's Slumber."

"Why would we want to share anything with them?" The AAU interjected.

"Our thoughts exactly!" snapped the UAA.

"Because!" Lo stepped in, finally resolved to do what she had set out to do. "I told your Queen and Princess I'd do everything I could to get them their drinking water by sunset, do you really want me to go back there and tell them her own colony prevented me from doing so?"

The AAU quieted down.

Then it was Lee's turn. "And I guaranteed the UAA Prince safe passage out of the nest before the end of the day. Should I be telling him otherwise?' The UAA ants shook their heads in silence.

"Then it's settled. Goldberg, Babak, let's go ahead with your plan. Everyone - let's get to work!"

So began an assembly of digging and drilling, earthing and unearthing, ploughing and piling. Some rested while others took over, then those rested while others yet took charge. Working together was not something either ant colony was eager to do, but given the circumstances, they saw no other choice if they were to complete their work before evening.

At first, the ants worked in stony silence, avoiding their rivals as much as possible. But once the dam started to take shape and peace seemed not so impossible a notion, the ants started to loosen up, help each other, and even make jokes every now and then. And though by the end, nobody would have dared call them friends, it seemed they had, at the very least reached a stalemate where they did not think each other so terrible after all.

As the sun descended behind the mountains, the dam stood ready, and the pond-puddle had been neatly divided up into two equal parts, with enough water for each colony.

Suddenly, as if the last gleams of light had set off alarm bells, the AAU Princess and the UAA Prince emerged from their nests out into the open, for the first time in weeks, and scuttled joyfully towards their share of the water. Then as their eyes met, they began playing and giggling as children do.

Lee and Lo saw this as their cue to give each other a big hug, nodding with a quiet understanding that all was forgiven. For a while, the other ants stood by, watching in muted disbelief for a while as the kids became the best of friends, then glanced at each other with new appreciation before calling it a night.

"Prince!" "Princess!" they called out simultaneously. "Time to go home."

Home. The word resonated in Babak's ears. He suddenly realised how much he missed being back in the pond, back in his cosy little abode. It may not have been much, but right now he would not change it for the chance to live in the most beautiful of castles or run off on the wildest of adventures.

But first, he had to make sure there was a home to return to. And that, they could only do once they had found the only person that could help them save it. They were off again at once in silent consent, every step, he believed, taking them closer the Old Woman Beyond the Sea.

Chapter 8:
The Big Storm

As days turned into weeks, an icy mist began to settle in the air. The Seaciatians were keeping to the dirt road, heading South as instructed, but even with all its curves and twists and bends, the Green Ruins seemed no closer than when they had initially started out. Since their food rations had run out, Lee would rise early in the mornings and gather whatever titbits she could find for them to eat, mostly berries, herbs or weeds. But as the Slumber months drew closer, little grew that could satisfy their hunger and journeying a day or two on an almost empty stomach was not too uncommon.

The days had become shorter, and sunlight was more a privilege than a given. But that did nothing to stop the team from propelling through the night if they had to. The chilly breeze of mid-winter was beginning to slow their movement, and the lack of humidity in the air made them long for water. Their moods were dampened, but their minds were all but deterred. Now, more than ever, they felt the fate of their home rested in their hands.

One day, when they felt they had travelled relentlessly past the humdrum grasslands standing unchangingly on their left for the hundredth time, and tedium of forestlands on their right for the thousandth, they finally stopped short when they came upon a looming, gnarled tree, the likes of which they hadn't seen before. Its bark was greying and peeling, and its branches hung limp and motionless, in stark contrast to the vibrant alloys of crimson and patchy brown leaves that remained strangely intact, soldiering through the winter's frost.

Awestruck, the frog gawked and gazed at the tree in contemplative silence. It was grand, majestic, and it was quite simply the most beautiful thing he had ever seen. Yet, he could not help the pang of sorrow gnawing at the pit of his stomach, for despite its unrivalled splendour, the tree seemed so crestfallen, so unhappy, that it appeared to be weeping in plain sight; sobbing tearlessly for a hundred years, yearning, perhaps, for a time long gone. The saddest tree in the world, the mice had called it, and it had certainly earned its title.

Nevertheless, it rekindled a spur of hope because being in the presence of this tree could only mean - and yes, there it was- just ahead, at long last- they had finally reached the Green Ruins.

It was a dell like any other, with one vital difference. It was utterly ravaged and dilapidated. But while the 'Ruins' part of its name seemed rather apt, if there had ever been any hint of green here, it had now been entirely engulfed by thick, unyielding shades of carbon black.

Barren trees with charred barks stood hesitantly, only half rooted to the ground. Remnants of peeled branches and severed boughs were splayed across the sooty floors with expressions of horror permanently etched into them. Heaps of cracked barks, charcoaled brambles, fractured pine cones, and wizened toadstools littered the dell, like relinquished bits of nature's past that no longer attributed anything to the present.

If the dell had ever been home to wildlife, those animals were long gone and were not likely to ever return to a such an unprosperous place. In fact, it held no signs of life at all, just a gritty, stifling reminder of death.

"*This* is it?" the frog managed tentatively, gulping, as they shifted closer.

No one cared to respond. They couldn't, in fact, as the display of the wasteland had momentarily rendered them all mute.

"What in the name of the Gods happened here?" Goldberg said finally to no one in particular.

Suddenly, the noise of debris cracking and crunching under their feet was surpassed by the loud sound of the wind's whistling. The sky darkened while they scrambled down onto a pile of rocks and descended into the Ruins. By the time they had taken a look around and found nothing but more decay and more debris, the whistling wind turned into an ominous howling, and the creatures exchanged glances with an air of concern.

"We should look for shelter," clamoured Babak over the howling winds. But before they could do so, a rumbling and roaring filled the air, and just when they glimpsed up at the thick clouds billowing like whirlwinds above them, the sky shattered and water started cascading down on them.

Though a welcome sight at first, after the waterless days they had left behind them, the torrent was heavier than their little bodies could handle, so they mustered up all their might and tried to resist its beating force, clustered together, and moved from side to side, looking for shelter.

"There!" shouted Lee, signalling a black hollowed log they could take cover in. They made a run for it, but they were slowed down as their feet, and the Mobile's wheels started to sink in the soggy soil underfoot. They hauled themselves out with some effort and made for the refuge. But it was no use; murky water was building up higher from the ground up, and before long, the log was soaked through by the time they had reached it.

Branches still rooted to trees began swaying and flogging the ground; one of which would have hit Lo squarely on the head, if it had not been for her strong reflexes to withdraw into her shell just before it did.

The grey sky was periodically lit by dazzling brightness as lightning flashed overhead.

The ground beneath them was beginning to flood, the current eddying and swirling forcibly around their feet, making them slip and topple over in the slush.

They made for the hill they had just clambered down to get to the Ruins, but the pile of rocks now towered over them, higher and steeper than they remembered it being just moments ago. They made attempt after attempt to scramble up to the hillock, but the rocks were too slick, making them impossible to clutch onto.

This was it, Babak considered. If there was ever a time when his froggy instincts had to kick in, it was now. He mustered up his strength and focused his mind and on the count of -one-two-three - he hopped!

Or tried to, at least. In his defence, he did manage to stay airborne for a few seconds before falling face flat into the mud.

"Stand clear!" cried Goldberg ready to show off his technological advantage. The goldfish pulled on some levers with his fins, and the wheels began to grow rapidly taller, unsteadily lifting the Mobile high enough to be at level with the terrain above the dell. "Quick, climb up!" he shouted over the teeming rain and growling thunder.

But just as the turtles and frog were about to oblige, a sudden gust of air punched at the teetering Mobile, thrusting it with the fish inside to the other side of the dell, and smashed it against a big trunk.

"Goldberg!" Babak, Lee and Lo wailed in unison, their voices quivering with fright. They tried to wade against the rising tides towards him, but the rain lashed down mercilessly, barring access. The currents thrashed them from side to side, and the water continued to build up to their heads.

"It's hopeless!" cried Lo, her head now half submerged under the grimy rainwater.

The three of them held hands, waiting for the imminent to pass, when all of a sudden, Babak caught a glimpse of a blurry flash of auburn, standing just above the rocks they had so desperately tried to climb moments ago. An orange tail flicked away the rainwater, and a small brown nose snuffled the air frantically.

"Hey! Over here! HELP!!" the frog bawled

with what felt like his last breath.

He was not sure the creature had heard him, and before he could try again, the muddy water had intruded into his mouth and nostrils, and he could not let out so much as another peep. Deep fatigue clutched him in a jolt and he relented. Everything went black.

***

Babak woke up on a rough surface in an enclosed space; location unknown. The walls were a jagged peeling bark, and the ceiling was covered unevenly with glow-worms, providing some light, but only barely.

Scrambling up to a seated position, the frog squinted in an attempt to get a better view of his refuge, but with his eyes stinging and his vision blurry, he could only just make out the furry outline of something or someone with a long bushy tail standing on its hind legs just ahead of him. The creature was leaning over a smooth ledge that jutted out of the floor.

Babak's eyes widened, trying desperately to get a better view. He opened his mouth to call out but a tremendous pain in his throat impeded it, and all he could let out was a hoarse sigh.

The animal turned around, exposing her twitching nose and a pair of round glinting black eyes that surveyed the frog slowly from head to toe. In her front paws, she held a notepad and pencil.

"You're alright," she remarked matter-of-factly, jotting something down in her pad.

"Where-" Babak began to cough out, but the burning sensation in his throat made him stop mid-sentence again.

"Don't speak," the squirrel admonished. "You are suffering from an acute case of throat trauma."

Babak was about to ask what that was when the squirrel glared at him and he shut his mouth just as soon as he opened it. He stared at her blankly for a moment, wondering how to communicate without putting further pressure on his throat. Not speaking was clearly not an option. He had to know what had happened.

Then he suddenly had an idea. He pointed at the notepad and pencil and made a writing gesture in the air. The squirrel grasped his meaning immediately, ripped out a blank page from her notepad and, walking on her two hind legs to where the frog lay, handed it over along with her pencil.

'*Where?*' he scribbled across the paper in squiggly letters as best as his trembling hand could manage and then held the page up for the squirrel to see.

"This is Diki's Dispensary - I'm Diki. This is where I tend to sick animals, like yourself," she said simply. But when he continued to look somewhat puzzled, she hastened to add, "We're in a hollow inside the trunk of an old oak tree. In a grove not far from the Green Ruins."

The frog gave a quick jerk of the head and hastened to scribble something else on the back of the page.

"*What happened?*" Diki looked over the frog's shoulder and mouthed the words as he wrote them down.

"You were caught up in the storm. You called for help, and I heeded your call."

That was when it all started coming back to him. Indeed, he had called for help, but he was almost certain he was not going to make it.

Suddenly, the vision of Dolores drifting lifelessly in the water gripped him, sending a shiver down his back. That memory spurred another as he recalled the last he had seen of his friends was worrying, particularly Goldberg who had been hurled to the other side of the dell.

He started to scribble in a frenzy; "*The others.*"

"They're all here," she reassured him before he could finish scribbling.

She clapped her paws together, sending the glow-worms scattering about the ceiling on command, revealing the entirety of the place whose outlines had initially escaped Babak's notice.

An opening in the bark that led to the outside revealed a now unthreatening and even pleasant starry night's sky. The storm had petered out, leaving behind only a cold drizzle and the scent of wet mud and boggy grassland.

Once he became more accustomed to the light, he began to appreciate the real vastness of the Dispensary. His eyes began to survey the room, and awestruck, he grew aware of the medicinal wonders that lay before him.

Across the room stood a sturdy wooden table, where Diki kept assorted roots and herbs and other ailments, neatly tied up in bunches and bundles or carefully inside labelled jars. On a smaller stand next to it, she had her medical equipment; needles, healing stones, and other novelties whose exact purpose only she was likely to know. To the left corner stood a kitchen stove, where a small fire had been lit, heating a small bubbling black cauldron over it.

On the side of the room where he lay, the frog was surrounded by about a dozen other wooden planks and ledges, jutting out of the trunk just like his, which served as beds for sick animals or insects, many of whom were now cooped up under leafy or petally blankets.

In the far corner of the room, the frog suddenly caught a glimpse of something familiar and somehow unfamiliar at the same time. A spherical crystalline structure was glittering faintly under one of the glow worms. He clambered to his feet to get a better look, in spite of Diki's stern gaze telling him to stay put. Could it be - yes, it was unmistakably the Mobile, but a cracked and disfigured version of it. Babak turned back towards the squirrel in alarm, his eyes wrenched large with fear for what might have happened to the scientist who used to live inside.

"Your friend is fine," Diki nodded towards the wooden bucket of water on the floor just next to the broken Mobile. The frog heaved a sigh of relief when he saw Goldberg curled up inside, sleeping in the corner.

"He was a little shaken up when I found him. I've given him a cup of herbal tea and he is now sleeping it off. That thing of his, on the other hand, I don't think I can fix."

She paused, then said almost to herself, "I'm not even sure what it is."

The squirrel scuttled off to her herb corner and took the boiling cauldron off the stove. She dipped a ladle into the brew and sampled it briefly before pouring some into a wooden cup and bringing it over to her patient.

"Here, drink this." She pushed the cup into the frog's hands.

He brought it closer and let the warm steam dressed in its tangy odour kiss his face. He took a modest gulp at first, feeling the stinging sensation intensify for a second as the roiling liquid travelled down his throat like fire, but he also noted how his throat began to feel much smoother and better almost immediately after.

"It's root ginger and sage, mixed with a few drops of tea tree oil," Diki explained. "Nothing artificial. I rely only on the healing powers of Mother Nature."

The frog nodded approvingly, and took another sip, before plodding over to the corner where Goldberg was resting in his wooden bucket. The goldfish looked so peaceful, his body buoyed up, rocking ever so gently in the water, none the wiser that his beloved invention was all but destroyed.

Now that Babak was more reassured about his friend's health, the frog let his feet carry him to other beds as he slowly examined the resting patients. Most, if not all of them, were rather small winged creatures with rounded bodies and black and yellow stripes.

Back home they were known as the Aristaeans; sky rovers, that were often spotted around the pond, dancing in an airborne buzzing band around the flowers for hours on end before they retired to their hives, which dangled conveniently from trees. There, they would spend hours making that viscous nectar, food that was said to be fit for both Air and Water Deities alike.

They always travelled by the dozen at least, and had a way of carrying themselves so majestically; their heads held up high, going about their day like nobody's business. That was if you watched them from a distance, but if you dared get closer, they might even seem like daunting creatures, as they would reveal their stinger in an intimidating fashion to make sure you knew your place.

But seeing them lying here now, so helpless and vulnerable, barely conscious or recognisable, shattered that powerful regal image Babak had always had of the Aristaeans.

Each bed had a sheet of paper attached to its front, detailing the patient's ailments. Most of them read *'Flower Poisoning,'* while others simply stated *'Unknown Climate Complications.'*

Babak mused over what it meant. He wondered why there were so many sick Aristaeans; whether there was a specific flower whose poison had brought this horrible fate upon the poor creatures, or whether the poisoning and the weather had gone hand in hand to make their recovery harder.

As he was surveying the patients, his eye caught sight of something which made his heart pound in his throat. In the other corner of the room, Lee and Lo were lying on their shells on joining beds, heads, and limbs dangling out inanimately. The vision of Lo struggling against eddying and kicking rainwater suddenly gripped him again, but then he relaxed slightly once his ears picked up the rather audible hiss-snoring unique to the turtle.

Horror gripped him again when he glimpsed a stream of dried up blood imprinted on Lee's shell. Terrified, he let his eyes travel up to the source of the blood; a fracture going deep into her core. They came upon her chart last, fixating on the writing: *'Deep fracture. Infection spreading. Remote chance of survival.'*

Suddenly, his vision faltered. The blood was rushing to his head, making him light-headed. His legs began to quiver unable to hold up the rest of his body. Black.

***

He woke up a few minutes later, tucked back into his bed. The squirrel was checking his pulse with her tiny fingers when he came back to.

Heeding the frog's imploring look, she began to relate what had happened to Lee.

"When I came out to save you, she insisted that I take you and her cousin up the tree first, while she swam out to look for the fish. A few minutes later, I saw her wading against the current with all her might, coming towards me, and she was not alone. Somehow she had managed to tie a long sturdy reed around the fish bowl and was dragging it behind her with her teeth. She tossed me the reed and helped push it up the tree while I pulled on it with some difficulty. When the bowl reached me, I briskly loosened the reed and tossed it back to her so she could climb up, but just as she was about to grab on, a vicious gust of air brought a severed branch thrashing towards her, tossing her into the distance. I knew I had no chance of finding her then as the mist was too thick and the wind was too strong, so I waited for the storm to lighten up before I went back for her. And when I did, I found her unconscious body sprawled across some black rocks a few feet away - in *that* terrible state."

Diki thought it best to stop there, but added almost as an afterthought, "She is quite a heroine. If it hadn't been for her, none of you would have made it out alive."

Tears welled up in Babak's eyes and began to trickle down his face. He gestured towards the notepad and paper lying on the ledge next to her, and she handed it over.

He quickly jotted, *"Will she live?"*

Diki considered the question gravely before responding. "I don't know," she admitted finally. "Her shell has been severely fractured, so she will need surgery. But I need her to be stronger before I can proceed. I will do whatever I can, I promise."

Babak was sure his heart had stopped

beating when he had heard those last words. A mixture of melancholy and guilt took over him. He felt so much awe and compassion for Lee. She put *their* lives first, and he was not sure he deserved this kindness from her. Not after having doubted her before. What if she didn't make it? How could he go on living with himself for having ever been mad at her? As thoughts of anguish raced through his head, he let the growing exhaustion and grief wash over him and he surrendered himself to the darkness of the night.

Chapter 9:
The Recovery

Babak awoke in a groggy state, with a notable absence of the burning sensation in his throat. He must have dozed off, he realised, then pressed two fingers gently down on his Adam's apple to make sure the pain was gone and feeling nothing, relaxed again.

He sat back up on his bed instantly when he heard a soft whimper. Eyes scanned the room, and there Lo was leaning over her cousin's bed, holding Lee's hand in her own, while weeping gently. Goldberg was awake too, swimming back and forth in his bucket in an agitated fashion.

Shedding his drowsiness, Babak hopped out of bed and scurried over to the turtle's side.

"Diki said she would perform the surgery now," Lo said jerkily, in between sobs. "She is not strong enough yet, but waiting longer would put her at grave risk." The tears kept streaming down her dejected face as she spoke.

Babak put one arm around her consolingly.

"What if she -? I can't; I won't-. I can't be without her," her voice trailed off.

The frog felt a stabbing pain in his gut as the words left her. He felt her pain, and he wanted to tell her as much but thought it better to compose himself and be strong instead.

"Where is the Doctor now?" Babak asked.

"Doctor?" Goldberg scoffed. "Barely. She is probably off chanting something to an earth goddess or doing a rain dance or something. Speak of the devil-"

Just then, the squirrel's silhouette appeared at the trunk's doorway. She strode in with a basket dangling over her lower arm.

"I was out collecting the last few ingredients," Diki muttered, taking out some muddy roots and plants from the bag. "We'll get started in just a few minutes."

"For goodness' sake, is that what you are going to use? Mud and petals? She doesn't have a tummy ache; she has a severe infection! We need science, not this Mother Earth mumbo jumbo," Goldberg remarked testily.

"With all due respect, Doctor," the squirrel began matter-of-factly, "while you've been busy inventing nifty gadgets that can't even withstand a bit of rain, I've been treating sick animals my whole life. This is not your domain, so please stay out of it."

Goldberg scowled but said no more. Diki proceeded to her medicine counter and with a round pebble, which was worn smooth at the edges, crushed the roots she had gathered until they were fine grains of powder. She then stirred the powder into the gurgling black-violet gob that was simmering over the stove.

"I will ask Mother Nature to bless the medicine now," she announced, then began chanting something in a high-pitched note.

Goldberg guffawed at first, then fell silent when he caught a glimpse of Lo leering at him pointedly.

"What is that, Doctor?" Dolores asked when the squirrel was done.

"This is a potent healing serum. I am

going to put a few drops into the patient's fractured shell, and we can only hope it will contain the spread of the infection. After that, I will piece her shell back together."

"I need everyone to chant with me this time. Follow my lead." Lo and Babak began to chant along in deep, resonating mantras. Even the scowling Goldberg joined in this time; nothing was as important to him at this moment as saving the turtle's life.

Doctor Diki gradually poured the serum into the crack in the shell. Lee's body jolted a few times, and Diki held her hand up commanding the others to stay back.

"Her body is reacting to the pain; it is to be expected."

After a few more jolts, Lee's body fell limp again, and her eyes remained shut.

"Now what?" said Dolores, fighting back a sob.

"Now, you wait over there while I see to the fracture."

So they waited all day, pacing to and fro in agonising silence. Once they were allowed back by her bedside, six pairs of eyes remained fixed and unflinching on the patient's composed face and her unmoving body for hours. Goldberg had also asked that his bucket be placed on a log to be able to see the patient better.

At night, they took turns watching over her, even though there was no real reason to do so. But they all felt more at ease knowing one of them would be there the moment she opened her eyes. They tried not to think about the possibility of her not ever opening her eyes again; the thought was more than any of them could bear.

It was already past midnight when Babak rose to take Lo's shift, but to his surprise, found her fast asleep on a stool next to Lee's bed, and Goldberg keeping watch instead. The fish appeared more sombre than he'd ever seen him.

"Poor girl, she was exhausted," said Goldberg solemnly, when Babak went to stand next to him. The frog could only begin to imagine what the goldfish must have been feeling at that moment. After all, it was his life Lee had been trying to save when she had taken the hit.

"Get some rest Doctor, I'll take it from here," said Babak more sternly than he meant to.

Goldberg looked on for a few more seconds, then relented and crawled up in a corner in his bucket.

For hours after, Babak stared on, transfixed on the frail sleeping turtle he no longer recognised; so calm and yet so feeble. Her hardened exterior had melted away, revealing the fragile girl within who just longed to stop fighting and be taken care of for a change.

He must have been standing there all night, when suddenly he saw her limp body beginning to twitch.

"Doctor!" the frog called out. The others stirred and gathered around immediately.

Lee opened her eyes slowly, but it took her a few full blinks to frame all her friends gazing down at her, enthralled.

"Slowing us down again, frog?" murmured the turtle faintly, smiling as best as she could. Babak never thought he would be so happy to hear Lee teasing him again. Lo, who could no longer hold back the tears, dropped into her cousin's arms at once, bawling.

"Lee, you're awake! I-I-I was so worried," she mouthed jerkily, in between sobs.

Caught off guard, Lee lay there stiffly for

a moment, but then relented and embraced her cousin.

Then, it was Goldberg's turn to praise the patient. "My dearest girl, you truly are a wonder. How can I ever repay you for what you did?"

Lee just continued to smile wanly, overwhelmed but also moved by their show of love.

Diki furrowed her brow. "Okay, let's try not to wear her out, she is still recovering," she warned, but couldn't help letting her lips curl into a gentle smile at the same time.

"Lee, this is Doctor Diki. She saved your life. She saved all of our lives," Lo remarked, eyes wide with admiration.

The patient looked up at her doctor with a deep sense of appreciation she could not put into words. "Thank you," her voice faltered.

Diki nodded gently in return. "Get some rest now,' she advised. "All of you."

They were so happy, they all gave Lenore one more gentle group hug, before heading to their beds. The Doctor stayed behind a little bit longer, to make sure the turtle really was fine, before calling it a night.

***

The team spent the next few days nursing Lee back to health. Lo, in particular, rarely left her cousin's bedside; she only did so when she went to prepare her meals, but even then she would hurry back with dishes overflowing with food and cups brimming over with detox juices. At first, Lee did not much care for being treated so vulnerably; she was stubborn at times, even refusing to eat or speak, but with the pass of time, she relented, let her friends take care of her, and even grew fond of all the pampering (though she would never admit as much).

And not just Lee. They all began to enjoy life at the squirrel's Dispensary.

Goldberg devoted most of his time to fixing up his Mobile, with some help from Babak of course, since he could not do much of the manual work from inside his bucket of water. Diki, intrigued by the Mobile's technology, also dropped in on their conversations every so often and lent a hand with what she could. In turn, Goldberg also passed some of his free hours learning about natural remedies from the squirrel. The initial tension between the two was beginning to thaw, and the fish proved more eager than ever to learn about the science behind herbal medicine (when he was finally ready to admit it was indeed science, that is).

Babak would also sometimes assist the Doctor with her other patients. He had started out by doing simple tasks, like providing them with food, water and other necessities, then later, when he became more confident in his nursing skills, he had even asked for the squirrel's permission to brew remedies on his own. He was developing a keen sense for healing and rather enjoyed helping to nurse sick animals back to health. It was nice to forget about the impending danger that threatened Seacity, for a short while at least.

Lee's strength was replenishing by the day, and everything seemed to be normal at last. And perhaps that was why the notion of their unsuccessful mission was beginning to weigh so heavily in their hearts. After all, they had gone beyond the flaxen-haired field and followed the dirt road, and it had taken them weeks to finally make it to the Green Ruins. Only to find it blackened and dishevelled with not a soul in sight.

They asked Diki to relay what had happened to the Ruins.

"There was a big fire there over two months ago. A big, black smog appeared overhead and suddenly caused everything to ignite. It was a few hours before the flames were put out, by which time the dell was practically reduced to ashes. Very sad indeed."

"What about the inhabitants? The animals that used to live in the Green Ruins, where are they now?" Lo enquired.

The squirrel shook her head gravely. "I'm sorry, but there were no survivors."

A moment of solemn sadness descended. A moment followed by many moments of dejection, fury, then despair, desolation and finally, forfeit. The kind of moment that ascertains that all that was renounced and everything that was sacrificed was in vain. The kind of moment when realisation dawns that the friendships almost destroyed, the lives almost lost, and the hearts almost broken was simply for nothing.

"Well, we've come this far, we can't give up now!" Lee broke the mourning silence.

"Lee, she's gone," Lo muttered, still crestfallen.

"You don't know that! She might have made it out in time. She's the mystical, all-knowing Old Woman Beyond the Sea after all, isn't she?"

"But what should we do? Where do we go?" Goldberg chimed in, still uncertain.

"We'll go around the Ruins, to nearby groves and copses. We'll ask every animal we meet until we find her." Lee was back, stronger and more determined than ever, and her optimism was contagious. So began the excited discussions about which paths to take and which to avoid the morning after.

It just so happened, one of the black and yellow Aristaean patients overheard their discussions, and the next time Babak was over at his bedside he told him as much.

"I know where she is. The one you call the Old Woman Beyond the Sea."

Babak's heart skipped a beat.

"How?" he managed.

"Like most other things in life, I came about her completely by accident," the bee began.

"The fields my swarm and I used to roam were being cleared away for months; meadows, flowers, and trees razed and demolished by ugly steel machinery to make even more hideous fume-sputtering buildings. One day, as we were leaving the hive, we noticed the air was heavier than usual, and the skies were thick with tendrils of black mist. Nevertheless, we hovered along our usual route and arrived to see that, to our dismay, the fields had been completely decimated. Everything was gone, not a single flower, weed, or even leaf remained intact. No use mourning its loss forever, we decided, so a few of us split up to look for the next, closest field to the hive."

"I flew out for miles, ventured here and there, left and right, but found nothing. I knew I couldn't go back empty-handed, especially as something told me the others had been unsuccessful in their missions as well. So I kept going for hours on end. After a while, I was so exhausted, I had no idea where I was. I could smell flowers a few kilometres ahead. So I hovered on with the little energy I had left, and what I found was absolutely beautiful. An orchard dotted with violets, daisies, lilies, and more; truly a floral paradise."

"I was so excited and tired and ravenous all at once, I almost headed for the flowers instantly, but a little voice inside of me told me to go back for my swarm first. I almost wish now that I had not listened to the voice, but conscience got the better of me, so I flew back in all haste to deliver the good news.

And, oh how they rejoiced when I led them back there! They danced their dances, twirled their twirls, each seducing a flower of their own choosing."

"Not long after, though, the swarm began to thin out. I had been too overjoyed and exhausted to notice it at first, but once I looked around, I saw far fewer bees than I had taken with me. I convinced myself I was imagining things. But every time I glanced up, there were fewer and fewer bees, until at one point, there were only about a dozen of us remaining. I broke away from my flowery embrace, to find the others."

""Hey, where did everyone go?" I called out."

"That's when I came across the most horrific sight. Every drone was lying on his back on the ground next to their flower, motionless. I was about to scream out for help when I felt a nauseating spell take hold of me as well and I made to rest in the shadow of the sycamore tree next to the orchid."

"That was when I heard her voice. "The field is poisoned.""

""Wh-Who's there?" I peered around, up and down but saw nothing and no one."

""Heed my words," she continued, undeterred. "Should you or any of your friends ever come to this field again, the price you will pay will be far greater.""

""Who ARE you? What have you done to my swarm?" I demanded, more testily than I should have. Because that was when she exploded."

"'WHO AM I?" she bellowed, and I shuddered all over."

""I AM ALL THAT ONCE WAS, AND ALL THAT SHALL BE.
BE GONE NOW. AND IF YOU EVER COME BACK, YOU'LL FACE THE WRATH OF THE OLD WOMAN BEYOND THE SEA!""

"Quakes were sent along the roots and branches of the tree as her final words left her. The voice must have been coming from somewhere inside or beneath the tree, but I didn't stick around to find out. I took to the air with what little strength I had left and flew as far away from her as possible, before the poison caught up with my senses, and I collapsed in the forest. Next thing I knew, I woke up here."

He paused for a moment, his expression

betraying his sudden concern for the frog who had so kindly devoted his days to nursing him back to health.

"You don't want to go there, mate, that woman is evil," the bee cautioned. "Just look at what she's done to us!" His eyes darted remorsefully around the room at the other patients, all of them from his swarm.

Babak's complexion was pale. All this time, they had been so intent on finding the Old Woman Beyond the Sea, they never contemplated that she might not want to be found at all, or the lengths to which she was willing to go to keep herself hidden.

He let his gaze wander over to his friends, dejectedly. They were in high spirits, unaware of the perils that awaited them. Lo was busy re-enacting stories from their adventures; she really had a knack for storytelling and acting, the frog thought. Lee was also in good health, enjoying herself, and contributing where she could with her screechy ant or squeaky mouse impressions. Goldberg and Diki were laughing and clapping and encouraging encores like any devout audience member should.

An endearing smile waned on the frog's

face as he studied his friends, pondering what it would be like if they could always be together; if they could always be this happy. It wasn't long until his expression hardened again, as he recalled how only a few days ago they had anticipated Lee never opening her eyes again. Lo's words echoed hauntingly in his ears, inviting an invisible knife to feel its way in the darkness to the strings of his heart and sever them with one swift slash; *"I can't be without her,"* she had said, and meant it.

He could not let that happen. He would not. They were happy here, and most importantly, they were safe.

Mind made up, he turned back to face his patient.

"Tell me how to find her."

Chapter 10:
The Old Woman Beyond the Sea

That night, Babak waited for everyone to fall asleep before sliding discretely out of bed. The restless glow worms rearranged themselves to light up his path as he grabbed scraps of bread, berries, and the crumpled piece of paper where he had jotted down some rough directions for his journey, and he shoved them into a bundled piece of cloth.

The next few steps were clear. What came after he arrived at his destination, he did not know, and did not want to waste time mulling it over at this point. First, he would need to get to the sycamore tree. The rest of it, he would just have to figure out after that.

He contemplated writing a note to tell the others what he was up to, but thinking better of it, he tied the bundled cloth around his wrist, cast a final glance around at his sleeping friends, and he tiptoed out of the tree house as quietly as the pitter patter of his feet obliged.

He grabbed onto the reed rope which had been conveniently left tied onto the bough. This must have been what Diki had used to haul the unconscious Goldberg up the tree the night of the storm, the frog mused as he writhed his little body down prudently and landing on the ground with a slight thud. Then, brushing himself off, and more resolute than ever, he set off under the cloak of twilight.

The night was pitch black, as if the full moon that penetrated the sky were squandering the light that it should have reflected onto the ground. The night was chilly but calm, and save a few disjointed branches here, and some damp twigs there, no trace of the storm that had almost cost them their lives a few nights previous, remained. That's the thing about near-death experiences, they swoop in unexpectedly and depart just as shamelessly with no regret for having changed someone's life forever.

The customary hoots and howls began to pierce the air. They might have once made the frog stop mid-track, if he were not so accustomed to them by now. Still, he knew that despite the darkness, one could never be too careful, so he made for the nearest expanse of tall grass for cover, then trod cautiously, letting his damp feet sink gently into the mushy pitted earth as he did.

And tread he did, for hours and hours, with no regard for time and all regard for purpose, until the first hints of daylight crept surreptitiously into the sky and thirst and exhaustion finally thwacked the traveller off his feet.

He quenched his thirst on some dew drops collecting on the careless weeds, then absently munched on his breadcrumbs and berries, with little notice for taste. In just a few moments, he was back on his feet again, sleeplessly ploughing through the stalks that kept striking his disconcerted face.

Flat grassland gradually turned into thick chocolate mud, and then a lumpy dirt path, which meant, according to the bee's instructions, that he was getting close. But still, he would have welcomed any clear sign that he really was on the right track; something perhaps more substantial than just a medicated patient's word.

His anxiety wore off at length when he turned a corner, skirted a dell, and as instructed, came upon a forked path. Instilled with hope, the frog uncrumpled the piece of paper in his hand, even though he had read the directions a hundred times over by now, to consult which of the two paths ahead carved the way to the orchard. But to his dismay, he found the writing on it had been blotted out, perhaps by the dew on the grass or perhaps by his own clammy hands.

"Remember, one path will take you to the sycamore tree, and the other will take you straight into a nest of hungry strays, and once they sniff you from the corner, there is really no escape," the bee had warned.

Panicking, the frog ransacked his brains in search for the right answer, but everything he thought he had known had escaped him at once, like air through an open vent. And to think, he had come all this way only to be led astray by his own incompetent mind!

"Come on, focus. Left or right?" His eyes darted one way, then the other. But it was no use.

He could not just go on standing there either; he had to choose one. He swallowed hard, his heart hammering all over the place, as he pictured his dire fate, should he make the wrong choice.

"May the Water Gods be with me," he said finally, and closing his eyes, he drew deep breaths to steady himself and took one reluctant step forward. Then step by step, his quivering legs carried him to where the wind was more favourable. His body twisted and turned to the tune of his feet, shifting him further and further until a ferocious growling brought him to an abrupt halt.

"GRRRRRRRRR."

His heart sank. He had trusted in the protection of the Water Deities, and they had let him down. Or perhaps he had let himself down.

Slowly and unwillingly, he opened his eyes to find himself standing face to face with a beast; with an air of pompous satisfaction in his burning, red eyes, and his sharp fangs baring boldly. The frog wanted to move, he had to move, but his nerves kept his feet stubbornly glued to the ground.

The beast's snarls grew more jarring and alarming by the second, and the frog knew he had to muster all his might and hurl himself, head first, out of the way before the imminent attack, and just hope - *nay pray* - his feet would follow his mind's pleas.

So he leaped. And not a second too soon, as the creature had lunged his snapping jaws towards the frog at that very moment, and in his absence, now found his nozzle awkwardly entangled in some very conveniently located (or inconveniently located, depending whose side you're on) thornbush.

It yelped out in pain and anger, and the frog, when he opened his eyes and began to make sense of what had happened, saw his chance to make a run for it. He darted past the wailing creature as fast as his feet would carry him, which as it turns out, was very fast indeed when his life depended on it.

Once Babak felt he had left a comfortable distance between himself and his attacker, he stopped to catch his breath. With all the commotion, he did not even realise how or when he had left Winter behind and stumbled unknowingly onto Spring, where the sun seemed to shine more brightly, and hundreds of flowers swayed alluringly in the warm breeze.

And there, at last, the sycamore tree

stood; sturdy, lazy, uncompromising and ominous all at once, beckoning him from across the orchard.

"I made it!" he exclaimed, hardly able to believe his eyes. "Maybe the Gods were with me after all."

He made for the gap under the fence that enclosed the orchard. Like the deceitful sirens who threw the once-brave Odysseus off his tracks, the flowers called to Babak; they danced for him and enticed him, but the young traveller was not deterred. Breaking away from the sorcery that was their enchanting aroma and soft murmurs, he instead skirted each and every flower and strode straight up to the sycamore tree.

The tree's stern presence felt oddly out of place amidst the alluring orchard, as if it had been thrown in there as a last resort, or as if it had barged in on the colours and whimsically decided to stay as a way of contrast in spite of all protest.

Babak circled the tree's wide circumference, cautiously feeling the gnarled trunk with his fingertips, with the hope of finding a door carved into. But there was no opening anywhere.

"Hello?" he ventured, meekly at first. He waited. No response. "Old Woman Beyond the Sea?" he spoke again, this time a bit louder and more confident. "I need your help. My home is in danger. Please." Still nothing.

"HELLO!" he hollered, this time, unapologetically. The very branches and brambles would have shuddered at the sound, had the frog been bigger or his voice naturally more reverberating. And yet, it was not enough to elicit a response.

His expression hardened as he began to pace the floor. No, he had not come this far to be ignored. He tried climbing the tree, threw some rocks at it, he even began to claw fervently at the ground, hoping to find some hidden entry, something - anything - that led to her. But nothing worked.

Hopelessness shrilled, clanked and drilled through his head. It was ironic, really. He had survived the absolute worst of it; batted away every challenge thrown in his direction, even if only barely. He'd sloughed off all trepidation, braved through the night alone, and just narrowly escaped the snapping jaws of a vicious beast. And for what? To be disregarded. To be played and deceived by words carefully scripted and scribed on a scroll whose real validity he was beginning to doubt.

Visions of the Water Deities' tender smiles and baleful glares mished and mashed into cold sneering glances and leering judgement, until he had to let out a scream, to vent his fury for the first time. Those cruel, disparaging Gods that had made him lose so much and gain so little in return deserved every ounce of the frog's umbrage.

He let his body slouch onto the floor, downtrodden, and could not help casting his mind back, now of all times, to the comfort and safety of his home. "Home," he lingered on the word as if it tasted of lemon zest pies, maple wine and acacia honey. How he missed those carefree evenings he had spent in his little home, and how he missed the way the sunlight grazed the pond in the morning, highlighting the bluest sparkling sheen he had ever seen. And, oh, how he longed for the day he could feel the water brush up against him again and make his skin tingle; the luxury of just being able to drift aimlessly about, without a single fret or worry.

Tears welled up in his eyes when he

realised that day would never come. First one drop, then two, and then a cascade of them streamed down his face, undeterred.

In a haze of panic, he leapt up and started to pound the trunk with his fists and stomp the ground with his feet, furious and defeated.

"You are not just killing me, you're killing all of Seacity!" he wailed, at last, in utter despair.

Just then, he felt a rumbling and a trembling. The tree's branches shuddered, and its leaves rustled, and the frog froze.

"Who are you?" demanded a stern voice.

"B-Babak Frog from S-seacity," he stammered, forgetting his newfound courage.

"I came here to seek your guidance, my pond is in grave danger."

"Frog?" she probed, unconvinced.

"Yes," he managed, more confident.

A long pause followed, in which Babak dared not utter another word. Suddenly, out of nowhere, a tunnel of dug-up earth suddenly popped out of the ground next to the tree, paving a way under the ground.

Babak eyed the tunnel warily, measuring it up. What if it was a trap? What if she wanted him to enter only to use her witchcraft to close up the walls and then bury him alive?

Still, he contemplated, he was left with little choice at this point. So he crawled in and cautiously felt his way through with his hands and feet in the damp darkness. At a junction, the tunnel stopped going down, and instead carved a path that would presumably take him underneath the infamous sycamore tree.

The dimness was deterring him, slowing down his every movement as the tunnel grew narrower, but he continued as best as he could. But all of a sudden, Babak stopped with a thud and fell backwards. He reached out and felt ahead of him.

"Dead end," he whispered, incredulously. But how could anyone just carve out a tunnel leading nowhere? It made no sense.

A sudden stream of light seeped through the ceiling, revealing a crevice, which had not been there before.

He halted and listened as the sand walls around him began to quiver. The vault overhead slid open like a hatch, revealing a gaping hole in the tunnel's ceiling.

"If you are who you say you are, then by all means, hop in," boomed the voice, this time much closer than before.

Babak gulped, his heart pounding harder than ever. Of course, his *unfroggy* nature had to come back to haunt him at this very precise moment.

"B-but I never learned to hop."

The voice was unconvinced. "You have five seconds."

He swallowed hard. "Come on," he reassured himself. "You can do this. For Seacity." Then his voice lowered to a whisper so soft, even he could barely hear, "for Lo." His eyes were closed, his squat tense. He was pure focus. He let his mind go blank and felt an energy he had never felt before surge through his entire body. And suddenly, somehow, he was elated, both mentally and physically; he sensed himself in mid-air, and when he opened his eyes - Could it be? Was he finally hopping, like he was always meant to do? Yes - indeed, hop he had, at long last! And the moment would have been even more wonderful if he hadn't found himself landing in a gritty, enclosed cell.

Even in the darkness, with the only

semblance of light emanating from a tiny, crooked candle, whose flame looked like it could go out at any second, the place looked damp and murky. A silhouette of a hunched figure stood poised against one end of the craggy enclosure.

"I apologise for earlier," the shadow remarked without turning around to face her visitor. "One can never be too careful in times as dire as these."

Babak felt the anger surging in him, as he heard her calm tone; that misplaced and audacious calmness after having tried to kill him. But he fought the urge to ram into her and stayed quietly rooted to the ground instead.

Several minutes passed before the Old Woman moved out of the shadowy darkness to reveal a stoic expression, betrayed by her watery, tawny eyes and the furrows lining her leathery emerald skin. Babak was taken aback.

"You're a frog," Babak uttered, only half-certain. After all, aside from the rare few times he'd glanced at his own reflection, he had never seen a frog before. They all disappeared some time ago, or at least that is what he had thought.

"A toad, actually."

Babak just stared on blankly.

"You said you were from Seacity," she said finally, ignoring his transfixed gaze.

"Do you know it?" Babak managed.

"Once. It used to be my home," she croaked sadly. "They said I was the wisest amphibian that Seacity had ever known," her eyes lit up for an instant, before she solemnly looked down.

The frog was stunned. He had been led to believe no one had ever left Seacity; that he would be one of the first that would live to tell the tale, if he ever made it back at all. Well, no one except for that mad witch in those children's tales. What was that folk song again? The one about that wise amphibian who lost her mind?

The greatest she was, once the ever-so-wise, before she went mad and decided to rise, and that's where she met her awful demise.

"Beltogra the loon!" Babak exclaimed.

"Err yes, that's me, I suppose. Good to see the Seacitians speak so fondly of me," she said with a sarcastic air.

Babak looked down at his feet in shame, when he realised how unwittingly rude he had been.

"But why would the Gods' prophecy lead us to you?" he spoke again, trying to change the subject.

"I suppose I owe you an explanation," she sighed. "Have a seat," she nodded towards a worn wooden stool by the corner, and he obliged.

"When I was a child," she began, "my grandmother used to tell me stories about a time before Seacity, where toads and frogs lived on the verdant fields, and drank from the running streams, while having chats with the mice, and squirrels and all other sorts of land animals. It was hard for me to even imagine such a place existed, because it seemed much more like a dream than a reality. But whenever I talked about going up and seeing it for myself, my grandmother would be quick to dismiss it. "Times have changed, Bell," she'd say simply, without offering much explanation on how and why this was so."

"So I put the idea out of my mind. I went on with my life in Seacity as best as I could. I studied hard and worked even harder to become the first ever Toad to be appointed Permanent Member of the Seacity Council. We amphibians always had a reputation for being carefree and easy-going creatures, but I proved them wrong. I showed them toads and frogs could do anything we set our minds to. My family was so proud of me, and all of this should have been enough for me to lead a happy life under the water. I had the praise, the admiration, the validation; but as the years went by and I got older, the image of that world beyond Seacity never faded away. The day my grandmother died was the day I decided to leave everything behind."

"I tried telling my family at first, but it was useless. My mother was convinced I was delusional; my father, that I'd been cursed. Of course, looking back on it now, I am not sure why I expected them to understand, when I hardly understood it myself. I just knew this was something I had to do. So despite all the backlash, or perhaps hardened by it, one day I gathered my belongings, and without saying another word, I disappeared into another life."

"The first sights of land were intoxicating and everything I had hoped for. But the more I travelled, the more I realised that what lay beyond was much less those lush, verdant fields or the sound of chirping swallows that my grandmother had told me stories about. Not a sound to be heard or a colour to be seen. Soot covered the grounds, grassland seemed to have combusted only to be replaced by rusty fields, like dust collecting on ancient relics on a shelf that had fallen out of use. A black cloud hung heavily where the blue sky should have been."

"All the while, my grandmother's words of caution, whenever she caught me daydreaming as a child, resonated with me, "You dream of a world that no longer exists, Bell.""

"As a young toad in a disfigured version of a world I didn't even recognise from stories, every ounce of me told me to turn back before it was too late. But I didn't, and more out of curiosity than bravery, I set out on a mission to find out what had happened to that other world; my grandmother's world. So I travelled for weeks, months, even years, looking for answers."

"Every animal I spoke to said the same thing. The green fields had existed once, my grandmother was right, but something was happening, and they did not know what, but what they did know was that it would not stop until it had consumed the entire world. Each and every one of their stories recounted different kinds of destruction; some about forests burning to the ground, others about toxic waste poisoning the lands, others still about suns burning too hot and withering everything in their path. But all their stories had one thing in common."

Babak let his mind wander back to the runaway tortoise, the travelling mice, the warring ants, all rendered homeless, one way or another. He recalled the dire, combusted state of the Green Ruins, everything smeared with ashy coal. Their words echoed in his ears as they each told their tragic stories. A mishmash of faces and voices, trills and squeaks and drawls, they all overlapped when pronouncing one entity.

"The black smog!" the frog shrieked, as it dawned on him.

"Precisely," the toad confirmed. "That was when I began to understand why my grandmother's generation had decided to take refuge in the depths of Seacity pond. I don't think they knew what was going on either, but they must have sensed the danger on land, and retreated to the least affected part and into the water in search for the safest possible haven. And for a while, I thought that was the best option too."

"That was, until I came across a group of travelling turtles heading West. They told me they were from Lakitan pond in the East. That one day, they had fallen asleep while basking in the sun, only to wake up to find the sky had turned an ominous black and that their pond was gone! The trees around them seemed to have been swallowed up as well. So they made haste and got away before they suffered the same fate as their once beloved home. That was when I learned water was not immune to the effects of the black smog either. I knew it was only a matter of time before Seacity suffered a similar fate. And indeed, with remote chances of survival, given most our inhabitants cannot survive outside of the water."

"So I went back to Seacity as fast as I could to warn everyone. But instead of being received with gratitude and honour, I was shunned and ridiculed. They said I'd gone crazy. They said I never should have left. They said Seacity was the safest place in the world, that it had been blessed by the Water Gods long ago, and that what I had seen on land must have messed up my mind."

"I stayed for days trying to convince my fellow Seacitians to take off, that the smog was coming, and it was coming for all of us. But all anyone ever said was that was impossible, that, even if that were true, the

Gods would warn us, that they would keep us safe."

"I knew that the only way to get through to them was to evoke the Gods. So I made up a prophecy, one that urged them to get out and see the perils for themselves. And I waited for years, for someone to turn up and find me in the Green Ruins. But I had to abandon my home there too, when the smog came and burnt everything down. I had given up all hope that anyone would come. And came you did, at long last. But I am afraid it is too late."

"You mean, the pond is already gone?" Babak swallowed the iron fist in his throat.

"Perhaps, but even if not, it certainly will be by the end of the Great Slumber."

The Great Slumber! Babak had forgotten all about it. On the first day of snowfall in the Winter season, the animals of Seacity would drop into a deep sleep until the advent of Spring. Once they gave into the season's sleep, however, there was no way to reach them. It was hard to tell when the Slumber would begin this winter, but given the increasingly frosty weather, it could be any day now.'

"Can the smog be stopped?" asked the anxious frog.

"Once, maybe it could've been. Before it became so powerful and destructive." The toad shook her head gravely.

"There are those among the animal kingdom that wreak gradual destruction upon the world that belongs to us all. They unleashed that black smog and nourished it with their pollution and their constructions; they tore down our forests and contaminated our seas, and the smog grew stronger and more devastating. They put our lives and their own lives at risk only to feed their insatiable greed. And here the rest of us are, suffering the consequences." She spat the words out in an exasperated rush. "They could've stopped it once. But now, all we can really do is to try to outrun it."

Babak was distraught. He came here to save his home, not to run away from it, he wanted to tell her. So many questions circled his mind, but somehow the words refused to leave him, and if they did, they refused to jumble themselves up to form a coherent sentence. How could they even get all the water dwellers out in time? Even if they were to leave Seacity, where would they go? Would it be worth leaving at all if it wasn't safe anywhere anymore?

Before he could speak, a faint scream from the near-distance shattered the frog's thought sequence.

"Help! Babak!!"

Was that Lo? No, it couldn't be.

"What IS that?" Another familiar voice chimed in.

"It's here, you must go at once," cautioned Beltogra.

"Come with me," Babak offered.

"No. I would only slow you down. Don't worry about me. Just try to save them."

"Babaaaak!" screamed a few voices in unison now.

The frog made to jump down the hole.

"Remember never to let your guard down. Wherever you go, sooner or later, it will find you."

Her words echoed as the frog dashed back through the dark tunnel. In a matter of minutes, he was out of the tunnel and back over ground, back facing the sycamore tree. And there Lee, Lo and Goldberg were, frozen still and looking very distressed.

"What's happening?" the frog enquired, his heart pounding against his chest and throat all at once.

"Look!" Lee pointed. A thick, black smog was cloaking the sky over the grove they had left behind. Its tentacles spread wide, at once combusting everything in its way. It moved slowly, gradually, with determination, and once it had set the course for destruction in the grove, its eye turned towards Seacity.

Chapter 11:
The Way Back

"We need to get back to Seacity, right now!" Babak cried.

"What *is* that thing?" Goldberg asked, staggered.

"Something terrible will happen to Seacity if we don't start moving right now," Babak shuddered.

Their eyes widened, instantly grasping his meaning, and before they could ask any further questions, the frog started bolting towards the smog at full speed and ushered the others to follow.

Journeying back would take at best a few weeks, and that was only if they kept their resting time to a bare minimum. The smog had already set a course for Seacity, gradual as it may have been. And even if the team somehow managed to beat the smog back, there was something else that was working against them; the Slumber was only days away.

But Babak thought it prudent not to bring up the impossibility of the mission just yet.

The way back already betrayed signs of the impending Winter's Slumber. Trees and bushes stood bare and menacing, their brambles teetering in the murmurs of the cold, biting wind. Every blade of grass, every fern-frond, drooped for lack of moisture. The grass stalks were brittle, looking more like straw, and a thin coat of grimy ash was already beginning to settle on the open meadow. All colour was drained away from the land, save the crimson glow of the distant blistering fire that threatened to engulf the fields, and the poisonous smog that stalked steadily on, threatening to deny their resurrection.

The toxic stench of smoke filled their lungs, and the closer the Seacitians drew to the smog, the more their eyes watered and the more their throats burned. All except for Goldberg, that is, who was safely enclosed behind the crystal shield of his Mobile.

Flames were roaring and crackling; their tendrils crept and crawled up some of the tallest boughs and branches, making for the grove ahead. And in the midst of it, there stood the oak tree sanctuary, home to the squirrel Doctor and her patients.

"Diki!" screeched Lee above the sizzling of flames, horrified.

"We have to go back for her," said Goldberg.

"Then we'll split up," Babak interjected in between coughs. "Goldberg, you and Lee go to help Doctor Diki and the bees. Lo, you and I will return to Seacity and warn the rest about what is coming."

With a quick nod of approval, Lee and Goldberg were gone. Lo stood nailed to the ground, complexion pallid, as she watched her cousin and friend disappear swiftly into the hazy clasp of the fumes.

"Trust in your cousin, Lo," the frog offered consolingly.

A long silence ensued before either of them spoke again.

"What is going to happen to Seacity?" the turtle asked suddenly in a husky, disgruntled voice Babak did not recognise. Her eyes were still peeled on the fumes that Lee had run towards.

"It's - it's hard to say," the frog said uncertainly. "The smog is likely to destroy everything in its path. We need to get everybody out before it reaches Seacity or else-" he stopped short when he heard a sniffle and glanced in Lo's direction to see teardrops glistening on her cheeks.

"Oh Lo, please don't-" he moved to lay a comforting hand on her shoulder, but she pulled away before he could.

"Don't pretend to care now-" she snapped, bitterly.

The frog was taken aback. "Of course I care!"

"You left, Babak. We were a team, and you just took off in the middle of the night. Do you have any idea how worried I was? How crazy we all went looking for you until the bee finally confessed where you were?"

"But I did it for you-"

"For ME?" She raised her voice so fiercely it made Babak freeze. "I almost lost Lee. For hours, I thought she was as good as gone. But then, by some miracle, she came back to me, and finally, we were all together again. Only to wake up one day and find you missing. Losing the two of you within a few days from each other is not something I could bear. And you say you did it for *me*?" she demanded, as she fought back a sob.

Babak was still, his breathing was quiet. His heart thudded once, maybe twice, before falling silent as well. He wanted to speak; he wanted to tell her how sorry he was; how wrong he had been to put her through it, but the words felt heavy in his mouth and tasted bitter on his tongue, like muck glueing his lips shut.

Minutes may have passed, or it might have been hours before Lo finally tore her eyes away from the imminent smog. "We should go," the turtle set off, steadfast. Babak quietly followed behind, with his head hanging low.

All day and all night, they pushed and shoved through the dry, icy gusts, from forestlands to open fields, without so much as stopping to catch their breath. Night came for the second time, but they refused to rest, even if their bodies desperately cried out for it. Without their determination to push forward, no matter what, Seacity didn't stand a chance.

The flames burned bright at a distance,

and the smog was getting thicker as it moved ever so gradually in their direction, making the air they breathed in heavier. But worse still for the frog, was the silence. All throughout the journey, Babak had kept throwing glances in Lo's direction, trying to strike up a conversation, but to no avail. Nothing had felt quite so rotten as having made her cry, and he wanted nothing more than to tell her so. Even so (and though he would have never admitted this to anyone), he could not help the occasional skip in his steps or the sporadic hums under his breath. For hadn't Lo said she couldn't bear to lose him? Wasn't that reason enough to feel - even if only just slightly- giddy?

Under their aching feet, the ground began to feel stone hard, and when their pace slowed almost to a halt, all of a sudden, in their daze and exhaustion, they heard what sounded like a shuffling and a muffled squawking.

They stopped abruptly as if they had collided with a wall.

"What was that?" Lo spoke for the first time in days.

The squawking resonated again, this time

clearer than before.

The frog and turtle exchanged looks to make sure neither of them had imagined it, then reassured, turned towards the source of the noise.

In the darkness, all they could make out was the outline of what appeared to be a large bird. A few cautious steps closer revealed the poor creature was battling to pull its long beak free from a discarded steel can.

"Hello?" Babak called out timidly.

The bird's large, despondent eyes betrayed its suffering, even though it could not so much as utter a word.

The bird lowered its head pleadingly, and

Lo gripped the can by its corners and tried to pull it off unsuccessfully. Babak then joined Lo in her effort, and together, they tugged and hauled, but that only seemed to hurt the flinching bird even more.

They pondered what to do next, and Lo suddenly had an idea. For some moments, she disappeared behind some trees, and then she was back with some viscous substance covering her hands.

"It's tree sap," she answered the frog's inquisitive look. "We'll need to apply it around the beak and that should make it easier to pull the can off."

"Brilliant!" remarked Babak, hoping to use the situation to break the ice. But the turtle ignored him, and instead, made to rub the sap around the creature's beak. On her mark, Babak tugged on the can and presto, there it was! It slid right off, just as Lo had predicted.

Free at last, the bird sat face to face with them both with a relieved look on her face. "I can't thank you enough!" she trilled excitedly. "I have been stuck like this for days. My flock is already heading South without me."

Babak was just about to accept the bird's

gratitude when the moonlight bounced off her face, revealing the goose's fiery orange beak. A vision of that ravenous bird's snapping jaws in the pond gripped him, making his heart pump ice water.

"It's-it's you!' Lo – run!"

"No – wait," the bird entreated.

Lo, who neither understood what was going on, nor whom even at the best of times would not have been fast enough to escape such a chase, was so tired she could barely move at all. Seeing her non-reaction, Babak took hold of her hand and began to swiftly drag her away. The bird batted her wings in the air in pursuit, then swooped down to the ground in front of them, obstructing their passage.

"Hear me out. That day when I chased you, I was so hungry, I had not eaten for days. I don't usually eat amphibians or reptiles. I was desperate! I am truly sorry. Please – you helped me, now let me make it up to you."

Lo pulled her hand free from the frog's grip. "We need to get to Seacity pond urgently. Could you fly us there?" Lo requested.

'But-' Babak was about to protest, then fell silent when he caught wind of Lo glaring at him.

"Certainly, hop on." Lo did as instructed. The frog, still unsure, did not move.

"Babak, get on," Lo admonished. "This is our only hope."

"Please, just give me a chance," the goose implored.

Babak finally caved in and clambered onto her neck, though not without a few horrifying flashbacks to when he was clinging desperately onto the creature's plumage as she flailed violently in the air.

Lo and Babak both clutched firmly onto handfuls of feathers, and with that, the goose flew steadily upwards in a wide arc, then began its glide homeward.

Being airborne was different when he was not fighting to hold on for dear life, thought Babak. The cool gusts of air beating gently against his face felt liberating even, like he could just let the wind sever all worries from his mind and carry them away in whirls and twirls. Just for a moment, he closed his eyes, and let a peaceful hush uplift his consciousness.

Then, reality stomped his eyes back open, and the drifting smell of acrid brimstone made his nostrils burn. The smog was skulking closer and closer, leaving no more than a few hours' distance between them. He wondered how Lee and Goldberg were doing; whether they had made it out of the grove in time with Diki and the others. Worry gnawed at the pit of his stomach and did a few backflips before a familiar sight came into view.

Seacity pond looked as splendid as ever, gleaming and glittering like pale blue velvet, as if it were starkly immune to the impending danger at its doorstep. But before the two Seacitians could let out a celebratory cheer fit for a homecoming, sadness gripped their hearts; a common understanding that, if they stood any chance of survival, they would have to leave Seacity behind.

Within minutes, they were hovering above their beloved home. The water's surface stood still, with no ducks or geese in sight, and no bees or crickets in the surroundings. The smoke must have set off alarm bells, sending all animals fleeing. All except for the Seacitians, of course, who remained none the wiser in their watery dome.

The goose descended gently and parked himself on the grass on the side of the pond, and waited for the pair to hop off.

"Where will you go now?" Lo asked.

"I am going to head South, to look for my flock. A long way away, but I know the route, so if I fly all night, I might just be able to catch up."

Lo and Babak watched and waved as the bird flew off into the mist like a silver ghost. Then without uttering a word, they scuffled past turtles' rocks and were just about to take a plunge when -

"Lo!" Lee's faint voice could be heard from somewhere above them, almost entirely drowned by a resonant droning chorus.

They glanced up to see the sky dotted with sequences of yellow and black. Swarms of bees, clustered tightly together to form a flying platform, were carrying Lee, Goldberg and Diki suspended on top. They set them down on the ground next to Babak and Lo.

"Lee!" Lo embraced her cousin enthralled. "Are you alright?"

"We're fine, but look!" she gestured at Diki, lying unconscious on top of them.

"She's not waking up!" Goldberg exclaimed.

"She must have breathed in too much of the fume," Babak, who had gained some experience in First Aid from Doctor Diki herself, took over trying to breathe some air into her mouth.

He pressed down on her chest and tried once, and then again. No reaction. He tried a third time and again, nothing.

They were all beginning dismay when suddenly the patient opened her eyes and gasped for air!

The bees and turtles and fish all rejoiced, as the confused squirrel sat up and only slowly began to realise what had happened.

But just before Babak could join in the cheering, he felt a slab of icy water land squarely on his head. To his horror, he looked up and saw hundreds of dusty snowflakes casually dropping out of the sky, like crumbling confetti leftover from a decades-old new year's celebration.

They were too late. The Great Slumber had begun.

Chapter 12:
The Great Slumber

Without so much as a wasted second, the frog raced to the very brink of the pond and dove into the water. The turtles followed suit and dove in after him, in an almost synchronised fashion. The fish needed some time to switch his Mobile from land to water mode, and then to get shove over the brink, but it wasn't long before he joined the others, who were, by now, kicking their arms and legs, as fast as they could, through ice water to the bottom of the pond.

Glimpses of their underwater home began to take form. In the dimness, they could make out shapes of underwater dwellers huddled together. They were all fast asleep, with their hushed breathing making their bodies rise and fall rhythmically; a gentle rhythm that no amount of shouting or yelling was likely to disturb. Some of the Seacitians seemed well prepared, having set up their beds already in weeds and algae, while others seemed to have just dropped asleep on the bare ground in the middle of what they were doing.

Right in the centre of Seacity stood the Palace, regal as ever and ignorant of the fact that in a few mere hours it would cease to exist altogether. Lee, who was now in the lead, motioned towards it, and Lo, Babak and Goldberg followed.

The team fought back the urge to give into the hazy slumber that was beginning to lull them as well and, instead, paddled faster and harder right up to the Palace gates. They brushed past the dozing guards and headed into the halls. The God Dolphinus stood proudly in their way, wearing a fearless expression, though this time his eyes betrayed his facade.

The sight in the Throne room was no more hopeful. The waters buoyed up bodies of sleeping Palace staff, from councillors and knights, to jesters and chambermaids, showing no signs of life, save an occasional snoring or wheezing. Even Lee's pet snail Dumbbell, or a rather bigger and rounder version of him (after weeks of chowing down all those meals meant for the presumably sick Princess) was curled up into a fat ball at the foot of the grand Throne, drooling shamelessly, while dreaming those happy dreams only snails know how to dream.

"We're too late!" Lo exclaimed, crestfallen.

"This is rather odd," Goldberg mused glancing around. "It seems they were caught off guard. Could it be the Slumber came early this year?"

"Where is uncle?" asked Lee, noticing the King's empty throne.

They exchanged quick glances, then rushed up the stairs to the King's chamber, and there he was, neatly tucked in under the covers of a king-sized bed. His head and limbs dangled out nonchalantly, and his mouth salivated as, his raucous snores, matched only by his daughter's, resounded beyond the chamber.

"Father!" Lo called out. "Wake up!" No reaction. After all, it was virtually impossible to wake the Seacitians from the Great Slumber once it had begun.

She knocked on his shell, shook him, even gently slapped him across the face, but the King would not wake.

"It's no use, Lo," Lee said, laying a hand on her shoulder consolingly.

"But why aren't *we* affected then?" Lo asked.

"Oh, we will be," cut in Goldberg, who had done some research on the matter. "It seems, however, that having just been outside, it will take some time for our bodies to adapt to this new temperature of the water. But once it does-"

"Zzzzzzzzzz," the King's booming snore interrupted.

Goldberg cleared his throat irascibly, then added "Precisely."

They fell gravely silent, not knowing

whether to just give up and accept their fate.

"Doctor," Babak suddenly had an idea. "If we were to carry the Seacitians who can survive on land out of the water, would the shift in temperature wake them up?"

"Perhaps," Goldberg mused. "In theory, yes. But there is no telling for how long. And conditions differ for different animals, so we can't be certain."

"Then we'll start with them, and with their help, we'll carry all of the others out one by one," he said stoutly.

"Have you gone mad?" Lee said, perplexed. "There must be hundreds of Seacitians, if not more, and the smog is right at our doorstep."

"And what do we even do with them once they are out of the water?" Lo added.

"We'll cross that bridge later." Babak turned to Goldberg, who seemed more convinced than the turtles.

"Goldberg, get word to Diki and the bees. See if you can come up with a way for us to get as far away from the smog as possible when we rise with the others. Lee, you start with the Palace. Lo and I will search the rest of Seacity and gather up sleeping animals. Let's begin with the reptiles and amphibians."

"Well, I suppose it's worth trying," Lo said, more convinced than her cousin. Though she had still not forgiven Babak for leaving her behind, she knew fully well the situation required their complete cooperation if they were to have any chance of success. "And I know just the place to start." Lo led the frog back to the gates and cocked her head towards the pair of dozing newts. "They're quite strong. I'm sure they'd be of great help if your theory checks out."

Josie and Bosie. Babak shuddered. He took a moment to swallow his bitter resentment about the irony of this moment. Not only was he expected to save the lives of his former bullies, but to save their lives first, before anyone else's; that was the kind of thing cruel senses of humour were made of.

He glared at them, sleeping so peacefully, their eyes fluttering gently, almost as if in their sleep they had transformed into blameless, misunderstood children. But even when donning that mask of innocence, Babak could still hear their mocking taunts and relentless teasing, telling him he was too much of a coward to do it; and their cruel jeers and sniggers saying he would never amount to anything. He wasn't doing this for them, he decided, he was doing it for himself. He was doing it because he could; because he was brave; because he was like those heroes he'd read about; and because despite everything, he loved Seacity and he wished nothing more than to save it. All of it. Even them.

He gave the turtle a curt nod and proceeded to grab one of the newts by the arm while Lo clasped onto the other, and they sloshed swiftly to land. Lee scurried about the Palace halls and chambers, madly searching for other turtles. Even Dumbbell might have been of use, she pondered, though judging by all his extra weight, his speed would probably not meet the standards this operation required. So she let him snooze on for the time being.

"We need to split up!" shouted Babak, once they were back drilling through the water to the bottom of the pond. Lo nodded, and they each headed to raid homes, yards, schools and stores, grabbing hold of every other animal they could find, and dragging and shoving them to the middle of the pond for visibility.

The Floating Market drifted listlessly overhead, showing no trace of those bustling crowds on Mondays or the wafting odours exclusive to Seacitian delicacies. The library, too, appeared to have been abandoned in their absence; its desks and shelves zinging with rust and its books coated in thick layers of grime.

The frog allowed himself a moment of nostalgia as he examined their covers with his fingers. He had read those books so many times, and yet it seemed so long ago, he only remembered the stories in fragments. So much had happened since the time his biggest adventures were lived across the pages, he thought.

He exited the library and was just about to resume the search for the remaining sleepers, when he caught a sidelong glimpse of his rock, his old home. He suddenly remembered how cosy and warm it used to be, and how wonderfully he used to sleep there. How many times throughout their journey had he wished to be back home, sleeping in its tight embrace; he could not recall. And there the rock stood, only minutes away, inviting him inside.

His feet grew a life of their own, and against all logic, they enticed him towards his bed. The soothing temperature of the water lulled and deceived him, and nudged him to close his eyes. And just for a moment, he did. Because he was so tired. So very, very tired, that for once, he stopped fighting, and he succumbed, feeling a heavy force lift itself off his chest and hover off into the distance. Had he known giving in could be so gratifying, he would have done it long ago.

Babak. A sweet voice sang, like a lullaby composed just for him. *Babak.* It beckoned him; it told him everything was fine, that he had done enough, that he deserved to rest.

Babak. It was Lo, he could see her lips curling into a warm smile. She had forgiven him for what he had done, and he couldn't be happier. He ran towards her, opened his arms wide, but just as he was about to embrace her, she began to crumble right before him. *Seacity is dying, Babak*, she said hoarsely. *I'm dying.* And she was gone.

"NO!" he wailed. His breathing faltered. His heart throbbed and doubled in stabbing pain. But it wasn't over; he knew it wasn't. So he fought back, like never before. Against the lulling waters, against the Slumber, and against all laws of nature, because for *her,* he would even defy biology.

So he fought harder still, until his eyes finally popped open. He leapt out of bed, more determined than before and resumed saving Seacity.

By now, Lee had carried all the remaining turtles upward, sometimes in groups of twos and threes, and having deposited them, was now dashing back to Lo and Babak's aid. Meanwhile, the two newts and tens of turtles were beginning to stir, wondering who was responsible for awakening them from such a wonderful sleep.

Once Diki and Goldberg had briefly filled them in and invited them to glance at the calamity brewing in the skies, they had also dived in to help. The smog now stood a mere 30 yards away, crawling forward mercilessly, while shredding and roasting everything in its path.

Now that all the remaining fish had been assembled, the rescuers began hauling their dozing bodies up to land. Babak glanced left, then right, up, and down, and was glad to see all the waken animals with such resolve. Even the newts were pulling their weight, balancing three fish at a time (two with each hand, and one with their tails like lassos). The first part of his plan seemed to be working, at least. He could only hope Goldberg and Diki had figured out a way to retrieve the fish without risking asphyxiation.

The two Doctors had, indeed, discussed the best possible way to get all of the Seacitians to safety, sending some of the bees away to call their comrades, and others to gather any objects lying around the forest that could be used as small containers.

So, when the frog, turtles and the newts surfaced this time, they were met with tens of halved pine cones, crispy leaves dented on the sides in a bowl-like fashion, and hollowed chunks of logs, lined up along the edge of the pond, all filled to the brim with water.

"Drop them in here!" cried Goldberg. Obliging, they tossed the creatures, one by one, from the biggest catfish to the tiniest comet fish, right into the improvised containers. Once that was done, they raced back down for their next load.

The next time they surfaced, they glimpsed the ground dotted with hundreds, if not thousands of yellow and black bees. "My former patients. They have offered to fly all of us to safety," smiled Diki, clearly moved by the gesture.

Bunch by bunch, they brought up the sleeping fish and hurled them into the containers, while the Doctors shoved and dragged them onto the tightly-knit platforms formed by the awaiting bees.

Lee and Lo swam back to the Palace and up to the King's chamber, grabbed on to the old turtle's arms, and with some effort, lugged him away.

"Lee, you're back!" the King yawned, stirred by the motion. "How was the quest?" Then his eyes caught sight of his daughter. "Lo, what is this? You should be in bed, recuperating from your illness."

"Father, we need to get you out of here. We're in terrible danger!"

"Is that so? Well, I trust you to do what's right," drawled the King, drifting back into sleep again.

The smog was almost upon them; it was only a matter of minutes before it devoured the pond. Most of the animals were still in a deep sleep in the containers and none the wiser about what was happening around them. As the rescuers hurriedly put the remaining Seacitians onto the bee platforms, the smog moved even closer, only seconds away from scraping the edge of the pond. Lee and Lo helped place the King onto one of the bee platforms and hopped on to the next platform themselves.

Ripples and waves were beginning to form on the surface of the now creamy, frothy water, making it churn and boil and acidify.

"That's all of them. Let's go!" Lee yelled over the rumbling.

Just as Babak was about to join them, he heard a muffled shriek from inside the water.

"Mama?" a baby bullhead had awoken and was now caught in the midst of the ferocious waves.

"I'm going back for her."

"Babak, there is no time. We have to go, now!" Diki urged.

"You go ahead, I'll catch up." And with that, he dove back under, kicking and flailing viciously against the turbulence.

"What's happening, Mister? Where's my

mama?" the tiny fish asked, disconcerted, when the frog was close enough.

"You're mama's okay,' Babak reassured gingerly. "But we have to go, now. Please trust me." He extended a hand towards her. The baby fish hesitated, then conceded, extending her flipper, which the frog, in turn, grabbed a hold of and heaved as urgently as he could through the roaring waters.

The bees were already airborne when he reached the surface with the last Seacitian. The stench of scorched ashiness was wafting in the sky, making it difficult for the panting animals to gasp for air.

"Babak, take my hand!" Lo called out, reaching her arm out as far as she could. But she was already too far away.

"Turn back! He can't reach me. Turn back!" she screamed, anxiously. But the bees had already set a course, and with all the raucous, paid no heed.

This was it, he was going to be left behind! Unless -.

"Jump, Babak!" Lo bawled.

The frog braced himself, mustering up his energy. He had done it once before, and he could do it again. "Stay calm," he whispered to the baby fish, who was beginning to flop frantically through his loose grasp outside the water.

Holding onto the slippery fish by the whiskers, the frog made a leap for it, then lunged for Lo's arm. The turtle just managed to reel him and the terrified baby fish in. She pulled him into a tight embrace, both crying and laughing all at once.

The flopping fish was then placed inside one of the containers, along with her still sleeping mother, where she huddled close to her, finally at ease.

"Where will we go?" asked Lo, uncertainly.

"As far as we need to," Babak sighed.

Clustered together in a tightly-knit group with the slumbering animals in between, they hovered away from the decaying scene.

Crowds of fleeing birds and beasts were spotted above and below them; some hopping, some running, some flying, and all escaping the clutches of the black smog.

The way was gloomy and desolate. Fruitless trees and brambles stretched around them, and the moonless sky clung heavily overhead. The rescuers combatted to stay awake, despite the arrival of Winter, only if to catch a final glimpse of their beloved pond, before it was entirely engulfed by darkness.

Chapter 13:
The Awakening

Sunshine sliced through the leaves of an undergrowth, where a frog slept under a pile of white lily petals. And what an unusual place for a frog to sleep, unless of course, this frog had been subjected to unusual circumstances throughout his life, which later inspired a series of strange, lasting habits.

His eyes fluttered open at the sound of chirping birds flitting about in the branches.

"Daylight already?" he mouthed to himself in between yawns, reluctant to shake off that lazy feeling that came with staying tucked in until late morning. He took a few more minutes stretching and scratching, wheezing and gaping, before he finally hopped out into the open.

Green meadows stretched for many yards to his right and left. Violets sprung out of the fields, inviting bees to emerge from their hives and dance around them in choreographed routines. They were only rivalled by the dandelion seeds that twirled at a similar tempo in the crisp breeze. All sorts of animals, rabbits, field mice, turtles and newts, were seen skipping, hiding and playing jovially on the grass.

Spring had arrived at long last.

The Seacitians had awoken in their new home, a creek somewhere in the far North, and they were still struggling to get used to their surroundings. Adapting was not proving easy. After all, going from the stillness of the pond to that of an ebbing stream, however gentle, had its challenges. But overall, the animals seemed happy to be all together.

It had been hard to explain why they were where they were at first, particularly when they had woken up in these strange waters, with little to no recollection of what had happened. Not all of them had awoken during the great hustle, and not even a fragment had observed the poisonous black smog that had almost brought about their demise.

"Oh that! I thought that was a dream,"

some, who had begun to stir during the flight, had said.

But those who had seen the smog and how it had spread its venomous tentacles, those who had smelled the acrid smoke and felt its impending horror; *those* Seacitians had all vouched for the four heroes who had saved Seacity (because after all, they had agreed, the spirit of Seacity lived on in its people, regardless of where they werc).

Once the shock and anger and fear had worn off, all that was really left was praise. Stories of hardship, songs of bravery, and kind words of gratitude, even from those they had least expected.

"You disappoint me, Dolores," the King had shaken his head at first, when he had learned the truth about her fabricated sickness. But even *he* could not hold back the proud grin from spreading across his face at the thought of both his daughter and niece's bravery.

"Hey kid, thanks," Josie the newt had relented. "And you know, sorry about, you know..." Bosie had added, hanging his head in shame.

The frog had been so stunned by their

apology, he did not know what to say at first. There was a time, perhaps, when he would have held a grudge about the humiliation he had suffered at their hands. There was a time, he would have run and hidden himself to never face his former bullies again; a time, where he would have doubted their sincerity, thinking this was another coy to lure him in and embarrass him again at some point. But that time was gone. It was like a figment of a distant past; a past that belonged to someone who had not travelled so long and so far, someone who had not just escaped the clutches of death; someone who did not know the value of not just living, but surviving. That time belonged to someone who knew nothing about friendship or sacrifice.

It was this Babak, the new Babak, the bold, confident, and passionate Babak, who had decided to give his former bullies a gentle smile of forgiveness in response, and it was this new Babak who had really, genuinely meant it.

Steadfast, the frog now stood watching Lee and Lo out in the field with their friends, the travelling mice, helping them set up their stage for the new sequel to their acclaimed play.

Chance had determined they would spot the entire cast of actors down on the ground, somewhere along their escape route and fate had decided they should make their new home together on this creek. It was a good thing too, as, since their first performance that night, which seemed now so long ago, Lo had not stopped thinking about the theatre and had now become actively involved, designing some of the mice's costumes, while Lee had busied herself constructing a new stage for them from the brambles and boughs she had found lying about.

Babak's eyes wandered from the turtles to the two lead actors; a sturdy, quiet male and a beautiful, confident female mouse. They held hands and giggled like children, and had to be admonished by the squeaky Director to stay in character. If nothing else, at least the smog had brought Anoki and Anaba back together again.

Diki had set up a new Dispensary in a tree not far from the stream, and the bees had all moved their hive just above it for convenience. Though they were mostly cured of their flower poisoning, they were still required to pay regular visits to the Dispensary for checkups. Doctor's orders. The other regular visitor was, among all things, a land-trodding goldfish.

Goldberg's Mobile now had updates, like clasping and climbing features installed, making it easier for him to travel freely across all surfaces. Always eager to exchange scientific knowledge, the two Doctors had much to discuss, and now, more time to do so. Goldberg had even begun designing a wetsuit, which would enable his squirrel friend to visit him underwater, once it was completed.

Everything seemed to be well at last.

Still, the frog could not help those moments when his mind wandered back to the blackened dell, the scorching boughs and the devoured pond they had left behind. To this day, the smog's presence sent chills through his body, and he doubted that sensation would ever go away, really.

He thought about Old Woman Beltogra and casually wondered where she would be now. A sudden stab of fear made him stiffen, as he did.

What if she had not made it out in time?

He then waived the fear, deciding that was not possible; that *she* had been the one who had warned them about the smog, not the other way round.

Wherever she was now, Babak assured himself that she was safe, just like them. For now, at least.

The forest fire might have burned out, and the smog might have dissipated. And a long distance may have been left between the animals and their old home. But what if this was just the beginning? Were they really safe here, or were they just counting down the days, months, years even, until they weren't? Just as it had happened with Seacity, and just as it had in various shapes and guises for all the animals they had met along their journey, be it a drought, a flood, or a forest fire, *something terrible* always came. And *something terrible* would always come again.

"Babak, the play is about to start!" Lo called out, beckoning him to hurry up and take a seat beside her. Dozens of animals were gathering around, excitedly muttering among themselves. Word of the mice's talents had spread across the entire meadow.

"On my way," the frog called back. For

some minutes longer, he stood there, breathing in the springtime breeze, as images of the smog and fleeing animals flashed before his squeezed eyelids.

"Wherever you go, sooner or later, it will find you," Beltogra's words resonated.

He shook it off, as best as he could, and wedged them in the back of his mind, where he would recall them only when necessary. They had made it out. They were safe. And for now, that was the best they could hope for.

The frog stood up, dusted himself off and ran out to the meadow to join his friends, for what was bound to be the best performance of the year: *'The Tale of Anoki and Anaba: The Reunion.'*

THE END

About the Author

Elika Ansari has published over 100 reviews, articles and short stories. As a Humanitarian Professional by day, and a writer by night, she tries to focus her writing on globally relevant issues with the hope of one day making a difference, however small, through the stroke of the pen (or click of the keyboard). Ansari has lived in over 10 countries and currently lacks a permanent home, but writing often provides the safe haven she needs.

Acknowledgements

I would like to thank my family for always believing in me and for supporting me in every way they could.

Thanks to Olsi and Anastasia for capturing the story so beautifully through their illustrations.

I would like to give a special thanks to Adam for all of his support and encouragement throughout the entire writing and post-writing process. I hope you know how much it has meant to me.

Thank you so much for reading one of our **Middle-Grade** novels.
If you enjoyed our book, please check out our recommended title
for your next great read!

Pierre Francois: 5ᵗʰ Grade Mishaps by Lori Ann Stephens

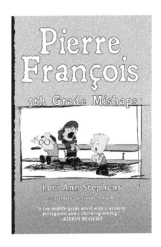

"... an entertaining story with the underlying theme of inclusivity."

–IndieReader